Brotherhood of Blood
Wildwood 1

Dance of the Dryad

BIANCA D'ARC

Copyright © 2022 Bianca D'Arc
Published by Hawk Publishing, LLC
New York

Copyright © 2022 Bianca D'Arc

All rights reserved.

ISBN-13: 978-1-950196-58-6

DEDICATION

To the voracious readers in my facebook group, which is called *The D'Arc Side*. You guys have really been there for me this past year and I can't thank you enough. Many thanks also to my dear friend, Peggy, who helps find the little bits of fun the typo fairy leaves behind during the editing process. Speaking of which, I would also like to thank my editor, Jess, for being such a good sport about editing a book during the holiday season.

And, as always, I dedicate all my work to my parents, who are both gone now, but who instilled in me a love for learning, for imagination, and counselled me to follow my dreams. My Mom famously told me to "Do what you love," when I was faced with a job offer versus my nascent writing career back in 2006, or so. And my Dad always said "Reach for a star. The closer you get, the better off you are." Both of them were much loved and are very missed.

PROLOGUE

Previously, in Wyoming...

Sally cradled Leonora in her arms. Her mate, Jason, was going after the shooter. The bastard had hit her great-grandmother with a silver bullet.

"Leonora. Talk to me. Tell me what to do." Sally tried to staunch the wound, but Leonora's blood was like nothing Sally had ever seen before. It wasn't red. The wound spilled sparkling, clear, sap-like fluid that smelled of chlorophyll and growing things. Leaves and light. The scent wafted to her, subtle on the night breeze.

"Silver may not harm you, granddaughter, but it doesn't agree with my magic at all," Leonora grumbled in a low voice.

"I lied before. I don't wear silver jewelry. It turns my skin black." Sally babbled as she tried her best to help Leonora.

"Believe it or not, that's good to hear. It means you have more magic than I thought," Leonora told her with a pained smile.

"What can I do for you?" Sally didn't know what to do for

a being like her great-grandmother.

Leonora was a dryad who was more magical than any other being Sally had ever known. Not that she knew much about the magical world she'd only just discovered.

"You must remove the bullet." The vampire's voice came from over Sally's shoulder. Master Dmitri had snuck up so silently, Sally had jumped a bit when he spoke. "You're the only one among us who is not poisoned by the silver. It might singe you a bit, but I don't believe it will poison you the way it would the wolves or myself."

"I see your point." Sally searched her mind for what little first aid she knew. She had a small pocketknife. She reached in and took it out of her pocket. "What about germs? Should I sterilize this?"

"Infection is not a worry. The silver poison that is already spreading through her body is. Time is of the essence." Dmitri sounded concerned. If a being as old and world-wise as he was showed concern, Sally knew she had to act fast.

She pulled the fabric away that she'd used to try to stop the flow of the wood nymph's sap-like blood. It tricked down her arm and the ground soaked it up like rainwater. Sally could see the silver of the bullet, not too far down inside Leonora's flesh.

Gritting her teeth, Sally probed the wound as gently as she could with the knife, coaxing the bullet out quickly.

"I'm sorry." Sally cringed as Leonora's body went rigid. A moment later, the bullet was out, and Leonora relaxed again. Her relief was evident, but her blood still flowed.

"Put the bullet in your pocket. Best not to litter the forest with something that could harm our furry friends," Dmitri advised. Sally picked up the bullet and looked at it for a moment before tucking it away.

"Such a small thing to cause so much harm." She looked from Leonora to Dmitri. "What now? She's still bleeding, and I can't seem to get it to stop."

Dmitri crouched across from Sally, on Leonora's other side. He took the aged dryad's hand and smiled gently.

"So, it is true that dryads bleed tree sap. I've always wondered." His teasing words brought a faint smile to Leonora's face, though her energy was clearly fading.

"Of course you have, old friend. But it is too magical for the likes of you. If you're tempted to taste, go slow. It could change you for all time."

"What can we do for you now, sweetling?" Dmitri was so tender with Leonora it brought a tear to Sally's eye. Could Leonora be dying? Is that why the ancient vampire was being so kind to her?

Sally wouldn't stand for it. Not when she'd finally found her great-grandmother. Sally had lost enough people in her life. She wasn't about to lose the only grandparent she'd ever known.

Sally called on her power as she'd never done before.

Wind sang through the leaves, whipping the forest into action. The branches of the willow under which they sat closed in around them, forming a canopy. A living, breathing, leafy green canopy in the night that blocked out almost everything. Only Dmitri and Sally hovered within, Leonora between them.

"I think your granddaughter is unwilling to let you travel beyond this realm just yet, my friend." Dmitri's eyes blazed encouragement. An unearthly light surrounded them all, painting each living thing within the dome of the tree in a hazy glow. Dmitri was outlined in red, Leonora in the purest golden green, while Sally's light was more toward the muddy end of the spectrum, a sort of olive green that leaned heavily toward brown. It was darker than Leonora's golden light, but it was no less powerful.

"Her light is that of the earth itself," Leonora whispered, pride in her tone as she took in the magic Sally had called. "It can heal me, but not quickly and not alone."

"Tell me what else I need to keep you here, Grandmother," Sally pleaded. "I'll do everything I can. Just tell me how. I know so little of my heritage."

"And yet, you've learned so much," Leonora said. Her

gaze was calmer now as the bleeding began to slow. "This willow will protect me while you gather the necessary people."

"People?" Sally was confused.

"Your family tree, my dear. You must find your sister and cousins. It will take a blending of all their magics with yours to bring me back. I can heal with help of the forest alone, but it would take many decades. If you can find our relatives and bring them here, together, you could augment the power of this wood many times over. For now, you must put me in the care of the forest. The willow will anchor my body to this realm while it heals. My spirit will float on the edge of this realm and the next while you fulfill your quest."

"Will you take the gift of my blood to help sustain you while you rest, Leonora?" Dmitri asked in a gentle voice. "Fair warning though—it could change *you* for all time as well." He winked at Leonora, bringing a faint smile to her face. One of her eyebrows quirked upward.

"An even exchange then? It's probably about time we expanded the bounds of our friendship to include that kind of trust."

Dmitri nodded gravely, the smile still touching his lips. "As you say, my old friend. I have long valued your presence in the woods near where I have made my home."

"And your empire," Leonora added with a weak grin. She was losing energy. Whatever they were going to do, they had to do it now.

Sally's power flared along with her worry. That seemed to get Dmitri's attention.

"Right. Let's get on with this so you can rest more easily," he said, his gaze moving from Leonora to Sally.

Lifting one hand, he shifted the shape of just one finger into a wickedly sharp claw. Sally felt the rush of magic in a way she'd never before experienced and saw the glow of red increase around his hand as he willed it to change. Before she knew what he intended, he used the claw to slash a fine line over his other wrist. Blood welled and he was careful to drip it directly into the wound in Leonora's shoulder.

From about twelve inches above, he dripped his dark red blood into the raw wound as Sally watched, dumbfounded by his actions. Leonora wasn't complaining, other than an initial hiss as the first drop sent up a sizzle as it began to react with Leonora's chemistry. Sally had to trust that these two magical creatures knew what they were doing. She was totally out of her depth where vampire blood was concerned.

Dmitri stopped at exactly thirteen drops. He removed his hand from over Leonora's body and licked at the remainder of blood on his wrist. When Sally looked at his wrist, the wound was gone. Not even a faint scar remained. Amazing.

When Sally looked back at her great-grandmother, Leonora looked better. Her wound was bubbling with pinkish light as her magical blood met and was aided by Dmitri's. She stopped fading though she was quite obviously still in bad shape. Even so, the effects of the poison seemed to have stopped in their tracks. She wasn't getting any worse, which was a huge relief.

"You'll understand my inclination to wait until you are completely healed of the poison to complete our exchange." Dmitri bowed his head in a formal manner.

Leonora nodded slightly, a faint smile hovering over her lips. "I look forward to the day I can fulfill my promise. For now, I must rest in the wildwood."

"And I will guard over your resting place by night, my old friend."

"The wolves will watch by day," Sally said without thinking.

"Already you speak on behalf of your mate?" Leonora seemed amused.

"I—"

"Don't worry. I approve wholeheartedly of Jason Moore. He's nothing like the creature my Marisol chose to wed. He's a good and honest man and you will do well with him. He will also support you on your quest, which could be useful. You two are a good match."

Sally was speechless. Leonora amazed her. She was at death's door and here she was reassuring Sally. Leonora was a trooper, that was for sure.

A tear tracked down Sally's face to splash onto the leaves that were hovering close. It sparked silver off the leaf. Only then did Sally realize the willow was weeping. It rained dew from its leaves onto Leonora, though none of the three within the circle of the willow's embrace were wet.

The silver sparkling dew was life. The tree's life force—perhaps the whole forest's life force—being given to the nymph who loved and sustained this portion of the wildwood. The dew landed on Leonora, and her body soaked it in. The dew seemed to be somehow preparing her body for what would come next, if Sally understood what it was Leonora wanted her to do.

"It's nearly time." Leonora's voice was fading as her own power ebbed. "You must deliver me into the willow. It will hold my body safe for as long as it takes."

Dmitri pressed a quick kiss to Leonora's hand then retreated a short distance. He nodded toward Sally, and she took his signal to mean that it was show time. Now, if only she knew what it was she was supposed to do.

"Speak the willow's name in your heart," Leonora coached. Sally held tight to her hand, disliking the way her skin had cooled. Leonora was in bad shape. "Ask for its help. Send it your power to help it do what it must."

Sally tried to do as Leonora instructed. She searched for and found the willow's name. How? She had no idea. She only knew that when she sent her thoughts spiraling toward the tree, she knew exactly what to say. It was as if some ancient instinct kicked in and took her by the hand, showing her what to do.

Sally kissed Leonora's hand, much as Dmitri had done, then moved back a few inches to let the willow do what it would. It was in the tree's hands—or limbs, rather—now. As she watched, feeding her power to the pliable branches of the willow tree, small tendrils snaked down from above and wove a complex pattern under Leonora's pale body. In no time at all, it had woven a sort of basket around her. Sally and Dmitri stood as one when the branches lifted Leonora off the ground, raising her to a standing position before pulling her into the heart of the tree.

She blended with the trunk in a flash of golden, green and pulsing brown light. A blend of her magic and Sally's, along with a hint of the blood red essence that Sally now recognized as Dmitri. The power flared to a high intensity. It was so bright, Sally had to look away. When she turned back, Leonora was inside the tree, suspended in the trunk as it slowly faded from crystal clear to translucent then to opaque.

Before Sally lost sight of her completely, Leonora smiled. She looked stronger. Happy in the embrace of the tree's ancient wisdom. Sally had touched its heart, its mind, and knew it would hold Leonora safe for as long as it took, sustaining her life with its own. With the life of the very forest around it, if necessary. It was her guardian now and honored to be so.

CHAPTER 1

The present day in Sacramento, California…

Sunny was doing a favor for a friend, teaching little girls in fluffy tutus about ballet. It was more about jumping around in pink tights at their age than the actual art of the dance, but they were so cute, Sunny didn't mind their ruckus. She could teach any class at this dance academy, as her friend had titled the small shop on the outskirts of an upper-class residential neighborhood. From these cute tots right up to the advanced ballet class filled with older girls, some of whom might have a real chance at a professional career. The academy was well-placed, and the owner had the right connections to get the girls seen by the right people in the arts world for auditions.

But her friend was at a business luncheon with one of those bigwigs and had asked Sunny to fill in for today, which she had done many times before. She enjoyed working with kids and teaching them what she knew. Sunny had gone to school for dance, back before the world had proved a bit too brutal for her gentle sensibilities. She'd earned a Bachelor of

Fine Arts in dance and was qualified to teach anything from tap to jazz to ballet. She'd even dabbled in ballroom a bit, though the competitive scene hadn't been for her. She just loved to dance. Anytime. Anywhere. For any reason. Dance had been her life for a long time. Until tragedy had struck.

Sunny had been in a car accident almost a year ago that had nearly ended her life altogether. She'd been T-boned by an out-of-control truck, and she'd had to be cut out of her own vehicle. She'd nearly died on the way to the hospital, but with good doctors, time, and a lot of physical therapy, she'd managed to walk again. She'd only just started venturing out on her own during the past week or so. Dancing to her old standard was still impossible, but she had regained enough range of motion to show these little ones the basic moves.

Sunny had tried very hard not to let herself get bitter, but being unable to move as she once had hurt deeply. She tried desperately to live up to her name and remain positive. Each day, it was a struggle. She'd lost so much. That car accident had taken her profession away from her. Until then, she'd been a principal dancer with the Sacramento Ballet. She'd danced in New York and in corps de ballet around the world, but she'd come home to her dream job with the company she'd watched as a little girl growing up in Sacramento.

That dream job was gone now, though she was still in her hometown and living once more with the family that had adopted her as a baby. Her parents were great, and they'd really been there for her after her accident. They'd taken her home to the ranch and installed her in her childhood bedroom, caring for her as she recovered. Without them, she would have been utterly lost. As it was, her career was over, and she was trying really hard to reinvent herself. Their support through it all had been fantastic.

Marilisa and Herman Stockton had been straight with her from the outset. They'd told her she was adopted when she was old enough to understand it. They'd loved her and protected her all her life, and she loved them in return, even if they were a bit odd. Quirky and kind of hippie-dippy, they were great people with a love of nature, music and all the arts. They ran a small art studio on the outskirts of town, where they taught classes in all sorts of art, particularly mixed media with found objects, which was one of their passions.

They were well suited to each other, having met in art school and married soon after. They couldn't have kids of their own, so they'd adopted Sunny and hoped she'd be an artist, like them. When she'd turned out to love dance, they'd supported her wholeheartedly and attended every one of her school performances, cheering with gusto for their little girl.

But they'd always been straight with her, and she respected them for that. Herman had been the one to break the news he'd gotten from her doctors that she'd never dance professionally again. He'd hugged her and cried with her when he'd told her, and then, Marilisa had come in with a bottle of wine, and they'd all gotten a little tipsy together. Her parents were cool like that, now that she was grown. They were more like friends than parents at this point. They were there for her when it felt like the whole world had turned against her.

Sunny's mind had wandered while the little girls leapt about the room in their pretty pink outfits. She schooled herself to pay more attention and went over to one little girl who had fallen on her little butt. Sunny bent down to help the child named Betsy back to her feet when the plate glass window at the front of the studio suddenly shattered and the mirror behind where she'd been standing cracked into a star pattern.

Everybody froze for a split second, and then, Sunny heard another crack from outside, and she fell to the ground, taking Betsy back down with her.

"Everybody lie on the floor. Right now!" she shouted at the stunned little girls. Luckily, there were only six of them in this class, and they mostly listened to what she told them to do. They were confused, but they all lowered themselves to the floor and began crawling toward her. That wouldn't do. "Crawl to the changing room," she told them as little pinging noises told her this—whatever it was—wasn't over yet.

Somebody was shooting at them! She'd learned what gunfire sounded like when she'd been dancing with a company in Israel. She'd also learned basic self-defense from her friends in that troupe and how to use a number of different weapons. Not that her peacenik parents knew anything about that particular skill she'd acquired.

The little girls were entering the changing room one at a time. Sunny watched as five little tutu-clad butts wiggled into the back room. Only Betsy was still in the open. Sunny prodded her forward, but she was trembling in fear, and Sunny had to take the risk of shimmying up to her and taking her into the back room at her side.

Sunny suspected the shots were aimed at her, not at any of the little girls, so getting close to Betsy put the girl in more danger, but the frightened toddler wouldn't move on her own, so it couldn't be helped.

When they were all in the changing room, Sunny kept them on the floor but looked over each one to make sure nobody was hurt. They were all okay, thank goodness, but Sunny wasn't sure what was going on or whether they were still in danger. The pinging noises had stopped, but it could be that the shooter was just waiting for someone to come out from the changing room to start firing again.

She had to, though. There was no phone back here and no way to get out of the building. Sunny was going to have to go back out there to get a phone and call for help.

"I want you all to stay here," she told the little girls. "In fact, I want you all to hide under the bench." There was a sturdy wooden bench bolted into the floor at the center of the room and the walls were covered in metal lockers. Surely, the metal would slow down any bullets, but if one got through, the heavy wood of the bench would be added protection. The little girls wiggled under the bench. There was plenty of room for all six of them under there, Sunny was relieved to see. "Now, stay there while I go make a phone call. Don't move. It's a game," she told them, and a few worried faces smiled tremulously at her. "I'll be back in a minute. Don't move," she reminded them and crawled back toward the doorway.

She really didn't want to do this, but she had to. Someone had to call for help, and she was the only adult on the premises. She peered around the doorjamb to see what was visible, and the first thing she saw made her gasp. There was a man out there!

A big man with an angry expression. He stilled when he heard her gasp, though how he heard that from yards away, she wasn't sure. His expression changed from angry to neutral as if he'd consciously flipped a switch.

"It's all right. I just came in to make sure everybody was okay," he said in a calm voice.

"I don't know you," Sunny said after a moment of deliberation. He had to know they were back here. The fact that he hadn't moved any closer counted in his favor, but he might just be waiting for her to step out into the open so he could shoot her point blank.

"No, ma'am," he agreed readily. "I'm Captain Dennis Palmer, US Army, recently retired. I was on the street when the glass shattered, and I saw you get the children to safety. The...uh...action has stopped, and the person who...um...broke the window ran away."

His hesitancy told her that he knew it had been gunfire, but he was probably keeping that information quiet so as not to scare the kids. Smart man.

"How do I know you're not the guy who broke the window?" she asked in a quiet voice. She was inclined to trust this stranger, but why she should do that, she had no idea. There was no reason to trust him, except that he had a kind voice and some instinct told her he was okay. Silly instincts.

"I'm not, but I applaud your caution, ma'am."

She peered around the corner, and she saw him pick up the broom they kept along the side wall. He began sweeping the broken glass toward the wall and away from the path the children would need to take to leave the studio. Sunny

12

glanced at the clock and saw that it was almost time for the parents to start arriving to pick up their kids. How was she going to explain this? The man continued to sweep up the glass, acting as harmless as possible. His physique and the way he carried himself told her that he was far from harmless, but as long as all that skill and ability was aimed in another direction, she was fine with him being there. In fact, he sort of made her feel a bit safer, though the shot-out window was definitely a reminder that violence had touched her life again today. For what reason, she had absolutely no idea.

The first parent arrived in the doorway, looking alarmed, and Sunny knew she had to take a chance and come out of the changing room. She stood and greeted the distraught mother with the news that everything was okay. The window had just shattered unexpectedly, and Sunny didn't really know why.

"Kids, I bet," the mother fumed as her little girl ran into her arms, unable to keep hiding under the bench once she heard her mother's voice. The mom scooped the girl into her arms and hugged her close. "The teenagers around here have nothing better to do than cause mischief. Is everybody okay?"

Sunny looked behind her to realize the other five girls had come out of the room as well. They were all potentially in the line of fire if the shooter hadn't really left the area. Sunny felt very exposed and really worried for the safety of the others.

"Well, I'm on carpool duty today, so I'll take them all home," the mother told her unexpectedly. "There's a big meeting up at the school about the budget proposal for the new gymnasium, and everyone else wanted to attend, so I told them I'd drive all the kids home today since I have the biggest vehicle."

Relief flooded Sunny. The little ones would be gone quickly and out of danger. Sunny saw the woman off with the kids and was glad to see them go, but that left her alone with the man. Captain Dennis Palmer. Hmm.

He'd kept sweeping up the glass, working quietly while the

woman had fussed over the girls. He had most of the broken glass in a pile in the corner and seemed to be looking at the window opening, sort of measuring it by eye. He pulled out a phone, tapped the screen a few times, then turned to her.

"I'm having a friend bring over a sheet of plywood and some tools. That ought to cover the hole until you can get new glass installed," he told her.

His practicality shocked her back to the matter at hand. "Oh, for heaven's sake. I have to call the owner. I can't really authorize any expenditures. I don't really work here."

The man frowned a bit. "No charge, ma'am. But I figured you were the owner. Sorry. My mistake."

"No, I'm friends with the owner. She's at a fancy luncheon to help solidify her connections in the dance world in this town. It's a meet and greet for the ballet company I used to dance with. I was just filling in for her as a favor," Sunny explained. "I'm sure she'd be willing to pay you. As long as it's a reasonable bill, of course."

"Of course, but I'm not really a contractor. I just saw this happen and didn't want to leave you in the lurch since you seem to be on your own here," he said with a friendly grin, reminding her that she was alone and kind of vulnerable here. She felt nerves run through her once more, but something deeper told her she was safe with this guy. It didn't make sense, but there was that instinct again.

"So, you're just a passerby Good Samaritan?" she challenged him with an answering smile.

"Something like that," he agreed. "If you know where a dustpan is and maybe a garbage can, I can get most of the glass off the floor. I suspect it's going to need a lot more sweeping to make sure every sliver is accounted for before they let the kids loose on it again."

"I suspect you're right," Sunny agreed, reaching behind the counter to get the dustpan and large bucket they kept back there, out of sight of the dancing space. She walked closer to the man and handed them over. "Thank you," she told him, pausing a moment and meeting his gaze. "Really.

Thank you for stopping and helping. I'm sorry to say that most people wouldn't these days."

He stood a bit straighter. "I'm glad I'm not most people then," he said with an amused twinkle in his eyes.

He really was a good-looking fellow. She'd noticed his physique right off. Tall, lean, muscular. Not weight-lifter bulky. More sleekly muscled, like a mountain cat. Though, why that image should pop into her mind, she didn't know. It just fit somehow. He had startlingly blue eyes that she found incredibly attractive. They sparkled with intelligence and curiosity and were set off by his sandy blond hair that was just a tad longer than clean-cut. He was beach-boy handsome, but he was definitely not a boy. Not by a long shot.

She would have thanked him again, but a truck with the famous Redstone Construction logo pulled up in front of the studio, and two men hopped out. They waved and went around to the back where they retrieved tool belts and a sheet of plywood.

"I thought you said you weren't a contractor," she accused gently, looking pointedly at the well-known logo on the truck.

"I'm not. Those are just friends of mine. Family, actually. My grandmother was a Redstone. The owners of the company are cousins of mine," he explained. "I knew they had a crew working in the area, so I just called in a favor."

Sunny knew about the work Redstone Construction was doing restoring a bunch of homes in one of the older neighborhoods. They'd bought a block of old houses, and instead of tearing them down to build something shiny and new, they had set about restoring those old gems to their original luster. It was the talk of the town.

"Handy," she observed as the two men came forward with the plywood.

They handled it as if it weighed nothing at all and smiled at her before covering the hole where the glass had been. She heard screws being driven home with power tools, and within five minutes, the empty window was securely covered, and the men hopped back into the truck and drove away. They worked fast. She'd barely gotten to say thanks before they were on their way.

"Now." Dennis had drawn closer, and the room was substantially darker with the big window boarded up. "Do you have any idea why someone was shooting at you?"

CHAPTER 2

Den had just about crapped his pants when he realized somebody was shooting at the little dance studio across the street. He'd staked out the place earlier that morning, hoping to possibly catch a lead on the woman he'd been sent to Sacramento to find. It wasn't his usual kind of gig. He was a soldier. Retired soldier now. He wasn't usually sent to find people. Like a detective or something.

The fact that the woman in Wyoming who'd asked him to take on this mission was, herself, an ex-police detective didn't count as much, to his mind, as the fact that she was the Alpha female over a group in which he sought to be accepted. The Wraiths were an elite military unit known throughout shifter culture. Den had worked with some of the men while they had still been in the service, but he was a little younger than most of them. Shifters lived a lot longer than regular people. Most of those guys were nearing their century mark and had tired of working within the confines of the human military long before Den had.

In fact, he'd only just retired recently. His inner cat had

been scratching at him from the inside out lately. It didn't want to be in the rubble of concrete jungles anymore. It wanted forest to roam in between missions. It wanted its own territory, even just a small patch of land it could call its own. Surprisingly, his inner cat wanted to settle down. Den hadn't quite been prepared for that. He'd thought his days of being wild and free—and unencumbered by a mate— were still in their prime, but something inside him, some deeper knowing, said that wasn't the case. And, when he'd gotten his first glimpse of the beautiful dancer surrounded by little angels in pink tutus, he'd known the truth.

If this woman wasn't his mate, he'd eat his combat boots. It wasn't just her looks, though she was gorgeous.

Her eyes were a lovely shade of dark blue, and her hair was honey blonde, with many tones from light brown to gold, combined in a way that no salon could produce. The many gleaming glints in her long mane of hair had likely come from the sun. She was also delicate in a way that almost frightened him. She had a dancer's frame—thin but muscular—but she also had an air of fragility about her. He worried for a split second that his wild nature would be too much for a woman like her, but it didn't matter to his inner beast. The cougar part of him had been thinking *mate* from almost the moment he'd caught sight of her.

Sure, it took a little more than just looking at someone to know whether or not they really were one's true mate. She definitely attracted him, but he'd wanted to get closer. To smell her delicate scent and perhaps, later, to taste her luscious skin. He wanted to know, desperately, if she could make him purr in human form. That, for big cat shifters, was the ultimate test.

He already knew she could make his heart stop. When the big glass window had shattered just as she bent over to help that little kid, he'd thought maybe she'd been hit. Then she hit the deck and ordered all the little girls to do the same, and he realized she was okay, at least for that moment. Thinking clearly too, which was also impressive. He'd have to remember to ask her where she'd learned such good responses to violence, though he was afraid he wasn't going to like the answer.

Den had gone on the hunt then. He'd stalked his prey—the bastard who'd opened fire on a room full of kids. He'd calculated the angles on the fly and figured the shooter had to be on the second floor of the building across the street. He'd pinpointed the window and had even seen the shape of the person's head just before the shooter took a few more shots and then ceased fire as the woman got the kids to safety in a back room and out of sight.

Den tracked the shooter. Their eyes met for a split second as Den concentrated on that open window, and then, the shooter fled. Den had bounded up to the open window, taking the fire escape as quickly as he could, but by the time he'd gotten to the window, the room beyond was empty, and there was a magical stench fouling any scent Den might have been able to track. Not good.

He could have tried to track the shooter at that point, but he probably wouldn't have been able to pick up the trail. Making a quick decision, he'd backtracked and headed for the dance studio. Sally, the Alpha female from the Wyoming wolf Pack, had traced the woman she was interested in to the studio through a paycheck dated the year before. It was a longshot that Den would encounter his target right away, so he had assumed the woman being shot at was the owner of the studio or some other employee.

He still had his mission to consider and would question the lady delicately about his target, when he had a chance. For right now, though, his inner cat was going a little crazy. It liked what it saw, what it scented, and what it all might portend for the future. If he wasn't getting way ahead of himself.

Which brought him back to the matter at hand. He'd asked her point blank why someone was shooting at her. The fact that his question didn't surprise or startle her meant that she knew it had been gunshots and not something else. How did she know what gunshots sounded like? Surely, in this quiet suburban neighborhood, she hadn't witnessed gunfire before. Or had she?

She intrigued him on every level. A woman of mystery that he wanted to puzzle out. That was another thing his cat liked. Puzzles. Damned if she wasn't hitting all his buttons and checking all his boxes. She appealed to both his human side and his inner feline. A dangerous combination, to be sure.

"I have no idea why somebody would shoot at me," she admitted, looking a little lost. "I just don't understand it."

"Do you know of anybody who has a grudge against the school, or the owner of the school?" he asked as gently as he could. He sensed she wasn't acting. She was truly bewildered and worried.

"Like I said, I don't understand it. I don't work here very often anymore, but I think Paulina would've told me if there was some kind of problem. She's an old friend."

"Paulina," Den repeated, as if he hadn't known the name of the owner before. "Is she the one who owns the school?" She was, he knew. All that information was in his brief. Sally had been able to find out a lot about the woman who owned the dancing school once she tracked the person she was looking for to it.

"Yes." Sunny looked at the clock on the wall. "That luncheon should be ending soon. I'd better call her and tell her what happened."

"I suggest you defer the phone call until you get to a safe location." He didn't want her to leave, but he could always follow her. Getting her to a place of safety was more important than spending more time with her, just now.

She looked at him with worry in her eyes. "Do you think they were really shooting at me?" She shook her head. "Don't answer that. There's no way you could know that." She reached behind the counter and came back with her pocketbook slung over one shoulder. "I think you're right. The window is boarded up, thanks to you, and there's not a lot more I can do here right now. I need to think, and I can do that anywhere. I'm going home."

He liked her decisiveness, but he was already planning to follow her. She might still be in danger, and he didn't want her getting injured—or worse, killed—on his watch. He'd picked up one of the bullets when he'd been sweeping. He hadn't touched it except with a napkin, but he suspected it was silver.

That meant whoever had been shooting suspected she was magical in some way and that she might be poisoned and incapacitated by a silver bullet. The thought made him grimace inwardly. Somebody was out to get her, and whoever it was either knew or suspected she was magical. Not good.

"I think your going home is a good idea." He couldn't think of any way to go with her. Not openly. There was no reason she should really trust him at this point. He had helped her, but he had to go slow. Being too eager would raise alarm bells and get in the way of his getting to know her better. "I am concerned, though. If I gave you my phone number, would you call me when you get home, so I know you're safe?"

Was he pushing too hard? He wasn't sure, but she looked at him skeptically, at first, then seemed to relent.

"You've done a good deed here today, Captain Palmer. Are you sure there isn't any way I can repay you?"

Oh, that was a loaded question, but he didn't let himself say any of the scandalous thoughts running through his mind. He had to back down and take things slow. She was only human. He didn't want to scare her off.

"You can start by calling me Den," he offered with a slight smile. She smiled back, and it was as if the sun had come out on a rainy day. She had a beautiful smile that lit up the whole room.

"Den. Thank you for helping me. And yes, I will call you, if you want. It's kind of you to worry about me." She reached for the pen and pad on the desk and gave it to him. "Write down your number for me."

He took the pad and pen and did as she asked. This was

good. She would call him, and then, he would have her number, and he would be able to back-trace her from there. They would talk again and perhaps advance the acquaintance begun here today. If he had his way, it would advance into something a lot more intimate, and a lot more pleasurable. When she called, he was going to ask her out. He'd already decided. No way was he going to let this one slip through his fingers. Something about her drew him, and he wasn't going to let her go. Not until he figured out the puzzle of her.

He handed back the pad with his number on it, and she ripped off the top sheet, sticking it in her bag as he watched. She looked up at him once that was done and smiled.

"I'm Sunny, by the way." She held out her hand expectantly, but he was frozen in place for a brief moment.

Sunny? What were the odds of finding two women named Sunny in the same dance studio? Zero. Those were the odds.

Heaven help him, but he had just found his target.

Sunny looked at the man quizzically. He was hesitating to shake her hand, and she didn't understand why. It was an awkward moment, but it passed in a flash as he seemed to awaken suddenly. He took her hand in his, and she felt a jolt of electricity pass between them. What the heck was that? Did he feel it too? Some kind of static charge?

In a day of things that didn't make sense, it was just one more. She retrieved her hand when he let go and shook her head slightly.

"Make sure you call me, Sunny."

She liked the way he said her name in his gruff voice. It almost sounded like a purr. He didn't look much like the barn cats on her family's ranch, but the sound of his voice held something in common with their vibrations. She didn't know why she thought that. Maybe those weird instincts again.

"I promise. It's the least I can do for how much help you've been to me." She looked at the boarded-up window. "Are you sure we can't reimburse you for the materials, at least?"

"No, thank you." He held up his hands, palms outward, pushing away her suggestion. "Consider it my good deed for the day. I'm just glad I was here to help."

"So am I," she had to admit.

"Can I walk you to your car?" he asked politely. Chivalrous. That's how he seemed to her. It was an old-fashioned word, but somehow, it fit him.

"It's not far," she replied. She'd parked in the lot next door. It was out in the open, so if somebody was still around to shoot at her, she'd be a sitting duck. Some of her worry must have shown on her face.

"That's okay. I'll just make sure you get to your vehicle safely. You lock up here, and I'll wait outside for you, okay?"

He gave her space, for which she was thankful. He really did fill up a room with his ultra-male presence. He walked out the door and waited just outside while she shut off the lights and closed up. She locked the door behind herself and took a deep breath before heading out of the tiny vestibule that sheltered the front door.

"I'm parked in the lot right next to the building," she told him as she began the painful process of walking the short distance. Her legs weren't quite as nimble as they had been, and her gait was a bit off, which made walking any distance somewhat difficult.

He set off, walking next to her, moderating his long strides to match her shorter ones. Thoughtful. She liked him more and more the longer she was around him.

"Did you hurt yourself when you hit the ground?" he asked, looking at her with concern. Darnit. He'd noticed her unsteady gait. She hated talking about it, but he deserved an explanation.

"No, I'm fine. I had a car accident about a year ago, and it left me a lot worse for wear," she admitted. "I've only recently gotten fully back on my feet and able to venture out on my own."

He shook his head, his lips pursed. "I'm sorry to hear that," he told her, and she felt that he really meant his words.

He...cared...at least a little about what happened to her. "Was there an investigation? Were they sure it was really an accident?"

His questions nearly stopped her in her tracks, but she was intent on getting to her car. Still, the thoughts he provoked were troubling.

"You think it might not have been an accident?" she countered, looking up at him from the corner of her eye as they walked side by side. She noticed he'd taken the side closest to the street, leaving her to walk between him and the buildings. Nice.

"Well, considering somebody was shooting at you just a few minutes ago, I'd be suspicious of anything that has threatened your life recently." He sounded so reasonable, but his words scared the bejeezus out of her.

"It was almost a year ago," she replied in a whisper. What if it hadn't been an accident? What if someone had really been trying to kill her? But why?

"And you've probably been surrounded by doctors and hidden away in the hospital or at home all this time. You just said you'd only just started venturing out on your own. Maybe whoever it was has been biding their time, waiting for you to become more accessible again."

"I really don't like the thought of that," she told him. "I have no enemies that I know of. No reason anybody would want me dead. It seems just too unreal that they'd wait a year for another shot at me."

"And yet, there were definitely shots fired at you today," he said gently. It was remarkable how calmly he was stating all these horrific ideas.

"If you're trying to scare me, you're succeeding." They turned the corner around the last building and were at the parking lot. Thank goodness.

"I don't want to scare you, but to make you think. I want to encourage you not to take chances. Not until you've figured out why somebody was shooting at you," he replied calmly as he walked her to her car.

"I have no idea how to do that," she admitted. "I'm not a cop."

"As it happens, I know an ex-detective who might be able to help you."

CHAPTER 3

Den hadn't meant to broach the subject of Sally quite so soon, but the perfect opportunity had just presented itself.

"Do you think your detective friend would really help me? What would something like that cost?" she asked, her voice low, but he could hear her. She sounded scared, which he hated, but if it meant she would seek help, then it would ultimately be a good thing, even if it grated on his inner cat's nerves right now.

"She would definitely help you." Sally would do more than help with an investigation if Sunny really was her long-lost sister. "And she wouldn't charge anything. She isn't in the business anymore, but she still has the skills and connections."

"A woman detective," Sunny said as if thinking. "I like that."

"I'll call her once you're on the road, and when you call me on arrival at your home, I'll be able to tell you what she said." He'd be following her home, but she didn't need to know that. "Maybe we could set up a video call with her so you can talk to her face to face."

"That sounds good," Sunny replied as they arrived at her vehicle. She stopped and looked at him as she paused by the driver's door. "Thank you again for all your help."

Den decided he didn't want to frighten her off, so he stepped back. His inner cat wanted to rub up against her, but he counselled the kitty to be patient. This was a game he intended to win, and he had to play it cool.

"You're very welcome," he replied with as much solemnity as he could muster. "Drive safe now."

She nodded and got into her car. He stood, watching from a few yards away as she started the car and drove out of the parking lot. He had his phone out and was already connecting the call as he loped easily to his bike, which was in the very same parking lot, conveniently enough. He hopped on, and the call switched to the headset in his helmet as he brought the engine to life and followed Sunny at a reasonable distance.

The Alpha male who led the Wraiths answered on the second ring. "Den? What's up?"

"I've made contact with Sunny. Someone was shooting at her, but they ran away when I pursued. There was a sniper's nest in the building across from the dance studio, and when I got there, they'd released some sort of magic that fouled the trail. Smelled awful. My nose is still clogged. Thing is, the sniper was using silver bullets. Sunny doesn't know about that, but she's scared. She was in some sort of car accident last year that's left her with long-term damage. She walks as if in pain, though she tries to hide it."

"Damn. Sally isn't going to be happy to hear that. She doesn't even know Sunny yet, but she's been going all big-sister protective already," Jesse reported, speaking fondly of his new sister-in-law.

Sally was mated to Jesse's brother, Jason, who was the Alpha wolf of the Wyoming Pack. Jesse was Alpha of the smaller sub-group of ex-military Special Operators known as the Wraiths, who functioned as a very elite mercenary group.

27

This was Den's first mission for Jesse. It was a sort of audition to see if he had the skills and was able to work under Jesse's command.

"Thing is, Sunny knew it was gunfire, and she knew to drop to the ground and get the little cuties she was teaching to do the same. She got them to safety in the back room by crawling along the floor. We need to dig into her background a bit more. Her instincts were spot on. Seemed as if she had experience under fire. Also, I sort of volunteered Sally to help her figure out why somebody was trying to kill her. I raised the possibility that the car accident might not have been an accident, and she seems amenable to talking to Sally as a detective, to help her try to figure out why someone's after her." Den got it all out in a rush, hoping he hadn't overstepped too far.

It really was up to Sally how she wanted to approach the woman she thought was her long-lost sister. She might not be too happy with the opening Den had taken on her behalf.

"Hmm. Well, that's one way to get them talking to each other," Jesse replied as if considering the problem. "I'll talk to Sally and see what she says. I'll have her call you direct. I assume you're following Sunny right now."

"You assume correctly, sir. She said she's only recently started going out on her own after finishing rehabilitation after the car wreck. Could be that's why someone's gunning for her now. Until recently, she was under wraps at home or in the hospital."

"Give me the plate number of her vehicle," the former Army major ordered. Den gave him the make, model, color and plate number of the vehicle. "She's headed out of town," Den reported.

"I'll talk to Sally and have her call you. We'll run the plates and get an address, but I suspect you'll be there before I can get that to you. Keep me posted," the major ordered and ended the call.

Den kept on Sunny's trail, allowing cars to come between them so it wouldn't look so obvious that he was following her. She didn't know her Good Samaritan had been riding a motorcycle, so there was no reason she would equate the bike with him. The traffic lessened until they were on a back-country road, and he had to stay well clear so she couldn't detect him. Nevertheless, he saw her pull onto a long driveway that led to a ranch house in the distance.

As he passed the driveway, he felt the distinctive tingle of magic. Somehow, the property was warded. No wonder the enemy hadn't been able to get to her until she started to go out on her own. There were magical protections around her family's home. And wasn't that a surprise? Was she aware of her inborn power? Was her adoptive family a bunch of magic users?

With more questions than answers, Den pulled off the road out of sight of the family's home. He wasn't leaving the area until he'd scouted a bit more closely, but first, he was expecting Sunny to call. While he waited, he sent a quick text to Jesse, giving him the address of the ranch and alerting him to the fact that he was already there, keeping it under surveillance.

Den's phone rang, and it was Sally. She didn't bother saying hello. She was too excited for that.

"You found her already?" Sally demanded, pure joy and surprise in her tone.

"It was luck more than anything. She was filling in for the owner at that dance studio today, but someone shot at her, and I offered your services as a detective to help her figure out why. I hope that's all right." If it wasn't, he was going to have to do a lot of backtracking, and it might ruin his chances of being accepted by the Wraiths, but he'd do what he had to do to make this all work.

"Of course I'll help," Sally answered immediately. "I want to talk to her. Can you arrange it?"

"I'm working on that right now," he replied, feeling relieved. "I told her I had an ex-detective friend who might be able to help her. She's supposed to call me any minute now, and I'm going to set up a video chat for you. Is that agreeable?"

"Perfectly," Sally replied at once. "Good work, Dennis. Thank you."

"You're welcome," he replied, glad that things were working out. "I'll be in touch shortly with the video call details." He spent a minute checking times when Sally would be free to do the video session, then ended the call. Sunny had promised to call him, and he was sweating it out until his phone rang again.

Sunny worried all the way home. She'd only just regained some modicum of independence, and now, she'd been shot at. She'd also met the most fascinating man she'd ever beheld and promised to call him. Sunny hesitated. Den really was a little too good to be true. Handsome, tall, broad shouldered with eyes that snapped with intelligence and humor. She liked everything about him, and that scared her.

Of course, even more frightening was the thought that someone was trying to kill her. She decided to trust her instinct that said Den was all right and placed the call she'd promised to make. She knew this would give him her phone number. A little more trust, but not too far for comfort. Not yet.

"Hi, Sunny." His voice when he answered the phone warmed her from within. "I'm glad you called. Are you safe at home now?"

"Safe and sound," she reported, feeling just the tiniest bit breathless talking to him again. His voice purred over her senses in a velvety wave of sensuality. "Did you get a chance to talk to your detective friend?"

"I did. She's free to video chat with you tomorrow, if you're available." They set the time, and Den gave over the information she'd need to connect to the call. Then, he said something unexpected. "You know, Sunny, I'd really like to see you again. Would you consider having dinner with me tomorrow night?"

"Uh…" She didn't know what to say.

It had been more than a year since she'd been on a date. Her last boyfriend, Alphonse, hadn't stuck around once her dancing career was over. He'd been a dancer too. He'd pursued her when it looked like they were going to dance together in the local company, but once she was injured, he'd found someone else, hurting her to her core.

Alphonse hadn't loved her as he'd claimed. He'd just seen her as a steppingstone to bigger roles and more clout within the company since she was a principal dancer. The bastard. She was still bitter about it, but this ex-soldier was nothing like Alphonse. For one thing, Den could probably wipe the floor with Alphonse without even breaking a sweat. For one moment, she imagined the scene but quickly banished it from her mind. That wasn't nice, even if Alphonse had broken her heart.

Den was still waiting for an answer, and she had to think fast. Didn't she deserve a bit of fun? Didn't she deserve a nice dinner with a nice man? Hell, yeah, she deserved it. She liked Den and wanted to spend more time with him. Sunny made her decision.

"I think I'd like that. Shall we meet somewhere?" she asked, her heart in her throat.

"We could, or I could pick you up," he offered. She wasn't quite ready to trust him that far. Being out in public with him was one thing, but giving him her home address was another.

"It's easier if I just meet you, I think. Where were you thinking?" she asked, trying to sound bright rather than wary.

"Have you heard of Arturo's?" he asked, naming one of the swankier steak houses in the city. She was impressed. She'd heard there was usually a waiting list to get a table there.

"I've heard of it, but I know it's hard to get a table there. Are you sure?"

"Arturo is an old friend of mine. There will be a table. I guarantee it." He sounded so confident. She shrugged and figured he knew what he was talking about. "Meet me there at seven-thirty. Just give the hostess my name, and she'll take you back. I eat there a lot whenever I'm in town."

"Okay," she agreed, feeling shy all of a sudden. "I really want to thank you again for helping me today."

"No problem," he told her, his voice rumbling over her senses, making her feel things she hadn't felt in a very long time and never this strongly. Never so soon, either. She'd only just met the man, and not under the best of circumstances. "Take care, Sunny. I'm really looking forward to seeing you again."

"Me too," she replied. "See you then." She ended the call without saying anything more, afraid she would give away how very attracted she was to the man by saying something stupid.

She hugged the phone to her chest for a moment, a smile playing over her lips as she thought about having dinner with the handsome captain. Then, she realized she was going to Arturo's. She had to figure out what she was going to wear.

An hour later, she had made a thorough mess of her closet, but she'd chosen her outfit for tomorrow night. Now, all she had to do was bide her time, and in just about twenty-four hours, she'd see the handsome ex-soldier again. She could hardly wait.

CHAPTER 4

When Sunny connected to the video call the next day, she was surprised to find Den on the call as well. She probably shouldn't have been so shocked. He was only being polite. He introduced Sunny to his friend, Sally, and Sunny felt a chill run down her spine. Not in a bad way. There was just something really familiar about the other woman.

Den was just as handsome as she remembered. That strong jawline looked phenomenal on camera, and his eyes twinkled with an energy that was visible even over the Wi-Fi connection. Sally was a beauty too. And there was this feeling of familiarity that Sunny just couldn't shake. The woman was as professional as Sunny could've hoped for and got right into the nuts and bolts of her investigation.

"I did a little preliminary research last night, after Den called me. He gave me your name and the name of the dance studio. He didn't have your last name, but that was easy enough to find from the studio's filings. I hope you don't mind. With that information, I did some database searches that didn't pop up any red flags except for the police report surrounding your automobile accident." Sally paused, and Sunny grew apprehensive. "The on-scene investigators noted a few inconsistencies, but nobody ever followed up. Judging by what I read in the report, it's just possible that the accident wasn't really an accident. I know Den probably mentioned that possibility to you yesterday. Have you had any further thoughts about who might want to kill you?"

"None at all," Sunny confessed. The very idea still bewildered her.

Sally's expression turned speculative. "It's also possible that they weren't trying to kill you, but to disable and, perhaps, capture."

"Capture?" Sunny's voice rose sharply as the implications of the detective's words came clear in her mind. Somebody was trying to kidnap her for heaven knew what purpose. "Like for ransom? My parents are artists. They're reasonably well-off, but they're not super rich or anything."

"There are other reasons for kidnappings," Sally told her with a grim expression on her face.

Sunny's imagination ran wild. "Like slavers or something? But wouldn't they want undamaged women for that kind of thing? Shooting me—or if the car accident was on purpose— I'd have been hurt badly if they captured me."

"For some things," Sally paused, her expression growing troubled, "it wouldn't matter what physical shape you were in."

Sunny couldn't even begin to imagine what kind of things Sally was talking about. She shook her head, drawing a blank.

"Sunny, this may sound odd." Den spoke for the first time since making the introductions. "Do you know anything about magic?"

Sunny squirmed a bit. Her parents were rather unconventional, to say the least. They did have some strange beliefs that Sunny knew weren't quite mainstream. Neither Sally nor Den seemed the hippie type that her parents usually hung around with, but maybe she was wrong.

"Um...my folks believe in some of that stuff," she

admitted somewhat vaguely. "Why?"

"Okay. Do you believe that there is such a thing as evil in the world?" Den pressed on.

"Yes, I do. You only have to turn on the news these days to see that evil exists," Sunny replied.

"Good point." Den nodded. "Well then, there are some people—evil people—who might try to capture someone, in any condition, in order to drain their power."

"But…I don't have any power. What kind of power are you talking about?" Sunny protested.

"Think about it. There are all kinds of power in the world," Den said mysteriously. "There are people who can see the future. People who can move things with their minds. People who can make things grow. And a lot of other weird stuff under the sun."

Sunny shivered. How did he know? *Did* he know? Or was he just fishing? Only her parents knew the things what she could do, and as far as she knew, they had kept the secret all her life. They'd counseled her often enough to never speak of it and never do it where she could be seen by someone else.

"Regardless," Sally interjected, changing the subject, "the fact is that the car accident could very well have been orchestrated to get to you. Likewise, the assault on the dance studio might have been a second attempt to get you. I would advise extreme caution. In fact, you might want to look into getting some protection."

"Like a gun? I already have one, but I don't usually carry it around," Sunny revealed. Let them know she would be armed and dangerous. She didn't really know these people, but her instincts told her they were okay. Still, she would be cautious. She didn't like anyone thinking that she was helpless.

"Start," Den said shortly. She frowned, and he explained, "Start carrying your weapon with you at all times. And whatever other protection you might have. I would suggest that you don't leave home unless you have good reason and a safe route mapped out. You might also want to acquire other kinds of protection, such as a bodyguard."

"I don't know if I can afford that kind of thing," Sunny said, thinking how outrageous it would be to have a bodyguard following her around. No, thank you. "And it would be weird. I'm nobody. I don't even know where to start to find somebody who could act as a bodyguard."

"You know," Den said slowly, "a very good place to start is with ex-military personnel, and it just so happens that I'm one. You know me. You could ask me how to find a bodyguard who wouldn't cramp your style or deplete your pocketbook."

Sunny didn't say anything for a moment. She wasn't sure about any of what he'd said. It sounded way too overboard to consider, but a little voice inside told her maybe it wasn't. She'd already escaped death twice, if these two relative strangers were correct.

"If that doesn't appeal, I could at least give you some pointers on personal safety. We can talk more about it tonight, if we're still on for dinner," Den offered, seeming to back off a bit, which made her feel a tad more comfortable.

"Yeah, we're still on for dinner," Sunny told him, though she wasn't sure if it was such a good idea after all.

Something felt a little off, though she didn't think either of these two meant her harm. If Den had wanted to hurt her, he'd had plenty of chances to do so at the dance studio. Her instincts said he was okay, and she couldn't really argue with that because she had no evidence to the contrary.

"I'd like to keep working on this, Sunny," Sally said after a moment. "If you permit. Maybe we could do another video call tomorrow, and I can let you know what else I've turned up."

"If you think it would help. I'm not sure I can pay you—"

"No payment necessary. I don't like to see good people being targeted. It rubs me the wrong way," Sally assured her. "I may be retired from the police department, but I still feel it's my duty to help where I can. This is just research, and frankly, I've got nothing more interesting to do at the moment, so I'm happy to assist in any way I can."

Sunny could hardly believe it, but the other woman's words rang true in Sunny's ears. She still had this overwhelming sense of familiarity, but she couldn't figure out why.

"Have we ever met before?" Sunny asked, unable to help herself. "You seem so familiar to me, but I can't place why."

Sally smiled, and her eyes twinkled. "We've never met, but ask me again in a few days, and I'll tell you all I know."

That was an odd answer, but Sunny didn't get any bad vibes from the woman. Quite the contrary. Sally seemed to be truthful in everything she'd said, and Sunny was pretty good at telling when folks were lying to her.

"Well...thanks for helping me. I really appreciate it. Maybe I can take you out to lunch as a thank you one of these days," Sunny offered. Surely, lunch was safe, and it might give her a chance to figure out why Sally seemed so familiar.

"Definitely," Sally said. "When you're out of danger, I'd love to meet you in person and share a meal."

Her smile was open and friendly, and Sunny found herself smiling back. Sunny confirmed the time she was meeting Den at Arturo's later that night and ended the call. She thought maybe something significant had just happened, but she really wasn't sure what it had been.

Den stayed on the video call with Sally after Sunny clicked off. He wasn't surprised to see Jason, Sally's mate and Alpha of the Wyoming wolf Pack, enter the viewing area as he sat beside his wife and put his arm around her. She had tears sliding down her face, though she wasn't crying heavily. She just seemed a bit...overwhelmed.

"Thanks for setting this up, Den," Jason said as Sally rested her head against her mate's shoulder for a moment. "I know it means the world to Sally." Jason's expression tightened. "But I'm really concerned about Sunny's safety. Two close calls are two too many."

"Agreed, Alpha. I'm keeping her place staked out. I'll be

following her to our dinner meeting." Den didn't want to call it a date in front of Sunny's sister, just yet. He was going to see where things led first before he made any declarations to anyone. "We're going to Arturo's, so she'll be safe as can be while there, and I'm enlisting a few of his men to help me guard her family's ranch. The place has a strong ward around it, but I'm going to go over the line, if I can, later tonight in my fur and do some reconnaissance."

"You're coordinating with my brother, right? Is he sending anybody out there to help you out?" Jason asked.

"Most of his men are on a mission right now, as you know, but I've got a Redstone Clan construction crew nearby that can back me up. Arturo and his guys also come under my cousin's authority, and they're more than willing to help me out on this. I've kept Steve Redstone in the loop. Jesse knows and approves." Steve Redstone had military experience and had served with Jesse. They went back a long way and were still good friends.

"All right. As long as Jesse approves, so do I. But tell me, Den, why do you want to join us rather than stay with your Clan?" Jason hadn't asked him that before. He'd let Jesse handle Den's request to join the Wraiths up 'til now even though Den had been friends with both Moore brothers for a very long time.

"As you know, Redstone has all sorts of shifters, though we're mainly cougars in the family. I enjoy the family, but I'm too fresh out of the military, and I don't quite fit in with the construction company anymore. They don't see much action except for the occasional dust-up. I want to use my military experience more than that, and there's nobody better than the Wraiths. I know cats and wolves don't usually mix, but I worked with a lot of Jesse's guys when they were in, and I have a lot of respect for them. I'm hoping they'll find me to be a useful member of the team, if all goes well."

That was almost verbatim what Den had said to Jesse when he'd first made contact and asked if there were any openings in the Wraiths for a Spec Ops mountain lion, just retired.

"Well, judging by your quick results on this mission, I'd say there won't be much of a problem," Jason said, nodding.

Den had to be brutally honest with Jason. "I wish I could take credit for the speed of this action, but really, it was just right place, right time. I got lucky in that the owner of the dance school had a luncheon and asked Sunny to fill in just when I got to town and began my surveillance of the studio."

"It was meant to be," Sally said, lifting her head from her mate's shoulder and wiping her cheeks as she controlled her emotions. "I firmly believe that there's no such thing as coincidence. I've seen it time and time again as a cop," Sally insisted. "You were meant to be there today to help her. Thank heaven. And thank you, Den, for taking care of her and watching over her. It sounds like she doesn't know any more about her heritage than I did, but someone knows, or suspects." Sally's voice turned cold and hard. "You said the shooter fouled his trail with magic. That says a lot."

Den nodded grimly. "It certainly does," he agreed. "I'll do everything in my power to keep her safe." It was a vow he would keep, no matter what.

CHAPTER 5

Sunny pulled into the parking lot beside Arturo's, feeling a bit odd giving her keys to her relatively inexpensive vehicle to the valet. The youngster didn't make any comment but took her keys with the same attention to detail he probably would have given any of the expensive luxury cars already parked in the spacious lot. Her car looked really out of place among them. She shrugged and walked up to the entrance, which thankfully wasn't far away.

She went in and gave Den's name to the hostess, who smiled warmly and led her a little too quickly toward the back of the dining room. Sunny scrambled to keep up with the young woman, not wanting to expose her infirmity in a room full of people, many of whom were openly watching her progress. When the hostess went through a door into another room, Sunny dutifully followed, glad to be out of the main room.

What she found beyond that door surprised her. It was a private dining room with a large table that could have seated a dozen or more, set only for two on one corner. Had Den reserved the private room just for them? What must something like that have cost? She hated to think of the expense.

Not that Sunny was poor. She was just frugal and hated waste. Ever since her accident, she'd had to be a bit more money-conscious than before. Her medical bills had been high, though her insurance had covered most of it. But being out of work and unable to return to her chosen profession had hurt her in the pocketbook more than she liked to admit.

She'd had to move back home, and thankfully, her parents had been more than willing to take her in. Thanks be to the Mother of All for her amazing adoptive parents, who were away this week on a retreat—the first time they'd left her alone since her accident. So many times in her life, they'd really saved her bacon. They were the best, even if they were a bit off the mainstream.

The hostess left Sunny in the room, and she took a seat at the table. No more than a minute later, the door opened again, and Den walked in. He came right up to her and greeted her with an outstretched hand, leaning in to place a kiss on her cheek.

It was a casual kiss, but it still took Sunny a bit by surprise. He was so tall and had such broad shoulders that, when he leaned close, he sort of crowded her personal space, but not in an objectionable way. Oh, no. She was more than happy to have her space invaded by the delectable aroma of him. Soap and fresh air and something wild and incredibly attractive. *Rawr.*

"Sorry I'm a bit late," Den said as he took his seat around the corner from her.

They were sitting at a ninety-degree angle to each other. Much more intimate than having the entire space of the table between them, she thought.

"You're not late at all. I just got here," she told him, taking her napkin from the place setting just to have something to do with her suddenly nervous hands.

"I'm glad. I try never to keep a lady waiting." His

mischievous smile invited her to smile back. "How did things go with the owner of the dance studio? Was she upset?"

"I called Paulina when I got home. She went right over to the studio after her luncheon, and I think she's got someone lined up to replace the glass tomorrow. She was upset, but as long as nobody got hurt, she was happy. I didn't, um…" Sunny hesitated. "I didn't tell her it was a bullet that broke the window. I figured that would only upset her more."

"Well, she won't hear it from me," Den told her promptly. "But I would advise you not to teach there again until you figure out who shot at you and why."

"Yeah, I realize that. I'm going to have to be a bit more careful about going out, which really stinks because I only just got to the point where I could go and do things on my own again," she admitted, though she wouldn't usually have been so forthcoming about her problems. There was just something about Den that invited her confidences.

"I realize that, but you must see the danger. People don't get shot at for no reason. Have you given any thought to that aspect?" he asked, pouring imported fizzy water from a glass bottle that had been on the table for them both.

"I have, and I still can't figure it out," she admitted.

She was saved from saying more by the arrival of the waiter. He was a handsome young man with impeccable manners. The way he deferred to Den was almost comical, but there was nothing overblown about it. Sunny thought the youngster showed great respect for Den, whom he clearly knew. He even addressed him by name and title. *Captain Palmer, sir.* The younger man had called Den that more than once.

He took their drink orders and set down a platter with bread and cheese that he had brought with him. Sunny had never eaten at Arturo's before but had heard about it from friends of her parents who had managed to get reservations. The bread and cheese platter was reported to be a standard prequel to what promised to be a spectacular meal.

As the young man left the room, another man entered. He

was wearing chef's whites, and he had a broad smile on his face. Den saw him and stood, smiling and holding out his hand for a brisk shake and a back-pounding hug.

"Good to see you, my friend," the man said, greeting Den warmly. "And who is this you have brought to my table?" He turned to look at Sunny, and she felt the impact of golden eyes in a handsome face.

"Arturo, this is my new friend, Sunny. She's been working with Sally Moore to research some things," Den replied somewhat vaguely. Arturo's dazzling eyes narrowed, but his smile stayed in place as he offered his hand to Sunny.

She gave him her hand and was both charmed and bemused when he brought her knuckles to his lips for an old-world salute. Was this guy for real?

"I have nothing but respect for Jason Moore and his wife. It's very nice to meet you, Sunny. I hope you'll enjoy your time here," he said, turning on the charm as he let go of her hand.

"Thank you. I've heard such rave reviews of this place, I'm certain I will," she answered honestly.

"Are you both feeling adventurous?" Arturo looked daringly from Sunny to Den and back again. "If so, let me send you a surprise selection. Lots of variety and a few things that aren't even on the official menu. All I ask is for an honest opinion on the new items after you're done. I'm trying out a few new things and considering whether or not to put them on the menu. Are you game?"

Den smiled widely, and Sunny figured it would be an adventure. "Sure, why not?"

"Perfect! Two new guinea pigs. The first dishes will be out shortly. I hope you're hungry." Arturo left, rubbing his hands together in glee. Den was just shaking his head.

"I suspect we're in for a treat," Den said as he sat back down at the table. "Arty doesn't make anything that doesn't taste fantastic. He's got a real gift."

"How do you know him?" she asked, curious at the contacts Den seemed to have.

"We used to play together when we were kids," Den explained. "We both grew up near Las Vegas and joined the military around the same time. Arty got smart and retired long before I did. He moved up here and started the restaurant, and I stop in and see him whenever I'm nearby."

"That's really nice," Sunny replied.

She didn't have many friends. Not long-lasting friendships like the one Den had just described. Sunny was more likely to have people flitting in and out of her life, like her parents did. They had many acquaintances. Students in their art studios and the like, but few true friends. They clung to each other more than anything or anyone else and seemed to enjoy things that way.

Sunny had never really formed the same kinds of deep friendships as the other kids in school, partly because she lived so far outside of town and partly because most of the other kids' parents had thought her folks were weirdos. That combination had caused a lot of the kids who might've been her friend to back off because getting together after school or on weekends was tough unless they wanted to come out to the ranch, and because their parents usually didn't want to drive them that far.

She hadn't really started to make friends until she started working. Touring with various dance troupes brought her into contact with so many different kinds of people. It was both fascinating and fun. She had friends all over the world now. Dance friends. Most of them didn't know she had been so badly hurt that she could no longer dance. She often wondered if they'd still be her friends if they knew.

Heaven knew, the ones in her hometown hadn't stuck around long after her wreck. Only Paulina had kept up with her and encouraged her. Paulina was a good egg, Sunny had decided long ago. One of the few people in her life, besides her parents, that she could count on.

"Penny for your thoughts." Den's voice came to her as she contemplated the vagaries of friendships. She shook her head, clearing her mind.

"Sorry. I doubt they're worth even that much." She chuckled, hoping he wouldn't press to know what she'd been thinking about. Some things were just a bit too private for a first date.

First date. That thought stuck with her. Was this a date? She suspected that Den thought it was, and she was more than happy to consider it that way, even after their unorthodox meeting.

"All right," Den said, relenting with a kind expression as he sat back in his seat. "One thing has been bothering me, though, and I really just have to ask you."

When he didn't go on immediately, she lowered her eyebrows and quirked up one side of her mouth.

"Okay," she finally said. "What is it?"

He sat forward, leaning his arms on the table just the slightest bit. "I want to know how you knew what gunfire sounded like and what to do when someone started shooting at you." He threw the questions down like a verbal gauntlet, and she had to shake her head.

"Is that all?" Sunny grinned wider. "It's no mystery. I toured with a ballet company and spent quite a few months in Israel during a particularly difficult time politically. I learned to duck pretty quick and what gunfire sounded like. That tour was a real eye opener."

"I'll bet," Den said, apparently satisfied as he sat back and sipped at his fizzy water. "I didn't realize you'd toured so extensively."

"Oh, yes." She went on to tell him about the many countries she'd danced in and the sights that had impressed her the most. He added anecdotes about some of the places they had in common, and before she knew it, the waiter was back with an array of dishes.

They talked and ate the most delicious meal Sunny could ever remember. She tasted everything offered, but it was Den who cleaned all the plates. She had no idea how one man could eat that much, but he seemed eager for each new portion that came through the door. The young waiter kept taking the old plates away and bringing new things for them to try to the point where Sunny couldn't really eat another bite.

Arturo came back and asked for their impressions of each dish. Sunny gave him her honest review that everything had been top-notch. She'd pointed out the dishes she'd liked even more than the others, and he asked pointed questions, seeming to take special note of her reactions. Den gave him his impressions as well, and Arturo left after sharing a glass of port wine with them.

Sunny saw that the bottle of port was from the Maxwell Winery in Napa, which was one of the most celebrated vineyards in the world. That led Sunny to suspect it was also exceedingly expensive. No mention of a bill was made after they'd had coffee and a plate of small desserts that Den mostly demolished. They simply got up and left, much to her surprise.

"What about the, um…bill?" she asked hesitantly as they walked through the main dining room, heading for the door to the outside.

"All taken care of," Den assured her. Unlike the hostess, he was walking slow enough that she didn't have to strain to keep up.

That was thoughtful of him, and she liked what it indicated about his care for others. It spoke of compassion to her. It wasn't anything flashy or designed to draw attention to how nice he was being or anything that would embarrass her in public. It was just a small unspoken gesture that showed without words what a nice guy he was.

CHAPTER 6

It was dark outside when they emerged from the restaurant. Sunny glanced down at her watch, surprised by how long they'd spent inside. The dinner had been so enjoyable from the food to the conversation to the company, everything had been amazing. She hadn't really noticed the passage of time, and it had been hours since she'd arrived.

The valet had run off to get her car for her, and Den stood with her, waiting for the young man to return. It was dark out, and the lighting in the restaurant parking lot felt intimate. They had been alone most of the evening in that private room, but somehow, standing right next to Den in the quiet evening air felt special.

The whole evening had been magical. Den had pulled out all the stops, treating her to a delicious meal at a popular restaurant that she had never thought she would patronize. He had shown her a little bit of his life and his friends in an unexpected way. It was clear he commanded respect from everyone in this place, but not fear. They respected him and liked him at the same time. And it was clear from the way he interacted with everybody that he liked and respected them as well. He had a kind word for everyone from the hostess to the waiter to Arturo himself to the busboy and the valet. He treated everyone well, and that spoke a lot about his inner self.

He gave every indication of being kind on the inside as well as the outside. Some people acted like good guys but turned out to be rotten to the core. Sunny had dealt with too many men like that in the past. These days, she watched carefully before forming any sort of opinion about a man's character. This one little dinner, as well as everything that had gone before with Den coming to her rescue in a potentially dangerous situation, made her evaluate him favorably.

He was the first man since her accident that she had been attracted to, and she was pleased to find that her instincts about him were running true. With her life the way it was right now, she couldn't afford to get involved with anybody of dubious character. She couldn't go through that again. She was through with heartbreak.

"I hope you had a good time tonight." Den's deep voice sounded from next to her, reminding her of the quiet night and the handsome man standing next to her.

"It was lovely. Thank you." She turned slightly to meet his gaze. "I can honestly say I've never had a better dinner, nor nicer company."

His smile was her reward. "I'm glad to hear you say that, and I feel the same."

They were completely alone, standing by the valet station at the side of the building, and the moment closed around them. Den moved closer, then closer still when she didn't move back in any way. Was he going to kiss her? Against all reason, she certainly hoped so.

His head dipped, eclipsing the light on the side of the building and putting her in shade, making the moment even more intimate. Then, his lips were on hers, and time stopped.

She felt the heat of him against her body as he drew her into his arms. He was so strong. Muscular in a way that was even more impressive than the male dancers she had known. Den was even more unconsciously graceful than the male ballet dancer she had dated so seriously before her accident. Den moved like a cat. She was nearly certain he had never danced in his life. Not in the professional sense, but he moved like liquid silk, and she had already noted and admired that about him. He was sensual in a completely unaffected way. It was just his manner. His thing.

And it stirred her senses to distraction. She could watch the man move for hours and be completely mesmerized. But the sexy way he moved paled in comparison to the way he kissed. Sweet lord in heaven! The man could kiss.

Sunny was completely under his spell. Time and space ceased to have meaning. There was only him. His lips on hers. His mouth possessing hers. His warm body hard against her.

Delicious. Every part of this encounter was a delight to her senses and warmed her in places that had been cold for far too long.

And then… It was over.

Den drew back and put space between them. Space she didn't really want. Not at that exact moment. But she was powerless to move. Her body had been seduced into a stupor, and it would take her a moment to get control back over her limbs.

Hoo boy! That man certainly knew what he was doing when it came to treating a lady right, as her mother would have said.

There was something…odd. She had felt it just before he'd ended the kiss. A tremor through his chest accompanied by a strange sound that somehow made her feel warmer still. She didn't know what it was. A growl? A rumble of desire? She hadn't experienced anything like it before, but it wasn't scary. On the contrary, she wanted to know more. Somehow, she felt it was…important. Though she didn't know why she felt that way.

Beyond all reason, and against all odds, he felt a purr rumbling through his chest. Dear sweet Mother of All. He had found his mate.

Den drew back, ending the kiss. His mind was awhirl with confusion and discovery. He'd found her attractive, but he hadn't really expected it to be so simple. Shifters often went a century or more without finding their mate. He was still quite young compared to most. Barely sixty, which meant he was still in the prime of his life and would be for at least two centuries or more, if nothing killed him in the meantime. With the uncertainty of a looming magical war, few people were certain of anything these days.

But one thing he was absolutely sure of was his unbridled response to Sunny. The person who could make a cat shifter purr while in human form was most definitely rare indeed. So rare that it was only a true mate who could do so.

Den silently blessed the young valet who must have realized what was going on and hadn't interrupted by arriving at the wrong moment with Sunny's car. As Den stepped back and released Sunny from his embrace, the car arrived seamlessly, or so it seemed. He might have liked a few more minutes to figure out what had just happened, but he was off balance.

The discovery of his mate had thrown him for a loop. He needed a few minutes to get his head back on straight and devise a strategy. For, he knew, winning Sunny's affection was something he was going to have to work to attain.

She wasn't a woman who would easily succumb to some passing charm. She had way more substance than that. If he wanted a lifelong commitment, he was going to have to prove himself to her. That would require a bit of strategy, a lot of prayer, and the blessing of the Goddess.

He wasn't normally a very religious man, but when it came to mating, he knew it was better to have the Mother of All on his side. She, it was said, was the one who brought mates together. If She had put Sunny in his life at this moment in time, then She deserved all praise and thanks. Den knew having a mate would change his life forever—for the better. That was an accepted fact in his society.

Matings weren't like human marriages. True mates couldn't be separated by the simple stroke of a pen on a legal document. They weren't a legal institution, but rather, a spiritual one that lasted their entire lives and into eternity.

The valet opened the car door and held out the keys to Den. He took them, sliding a generous tip to the youngster, who grinned back in delight then disappeared. Smart kid.

Den turned to Sunny and held out her keys. She took them, but he held on a bit longer, challenging her to meet his gaze.

"I enjoyed our time together tonight, Sunny," he told her, his voice rumbling with his inner cat, just barely suppressed.

"I did too," she replied, somewhat shier than he'd expected. "Thanks for everything."

"I'd like to see you again. May I call you?" he asked, trying to keep his wilder side under control and focus on being a gentleman. Sunny was too important to his future happiness to mess this up.

Her eyes flared with happiness, if he was reading her expression correctly. It gave him hope. He released her keys into her hand.

"Sure." Her cheeks flushed a little as her head dipped. He was enchanted by her response.

"Would it seem terribly old-fashioned of me to ask that you give me a call when you get home? I just want to make sure you get there safely." He would be discreetly following her home to be certain of her safety, but she didn't need to know that. He just wanted to hear her voice and solidify the connection between them before too much more time had passed.

"That's really nice of you. I'll do that, just to set your mind at ease." Her smile indicated her call would be more than just a safety check. He got the distinct impression that she wanted to talk to him again too. Sooner, rather than later. His inner cat wanted to purr in satisfaction.

She got into her car, and he closed the door for her. It was already running so all she had to do was put in gear and drive away, which she did, as he watched.

The moment she was out of sight, the valet reappeared with Den's bike and the leather jacket he'd left with the kid. Den put on his jacket, hopped on the bike, and followed Sunny home.

Her little putt-putt of a car meant it was easy enough to catch up with her. All he had to do was lay back and follow at a distance, to make certain she was safe. He had backup too. He'd had time to make sure enough of his skilled Clanmates were at Arturo's tonight to get a good look at Sunny as she walked through the dining room. They were going to help him keep her safe.

Although he was seeking to move to Wyoming and join Moore's Pack, Den would never cease to be a Redstone. He would never cut ties with the Clan where most of his extended family would remain for their entire lives. He just wanted...more. He had the Alpha's blessing on his desire to ally with Major Moore and become a Wraith. These days, the Packs and Clans were working more closely together, and beside that, the Redstone Alpha had long been friends with both Jason and Jesse Moore.

Jason led the entire Pack while his older brother, Jesse, was Alpha to the select group of ex-military shifters who had gathered around him. It was an uncommon situation, but it really worked well for them. Just like the five Redstone brothers. Normally, having five Alpha males at the head of the Clan wouldn't have been feasible, but for the brothers, it really worked. The younger ones all deferred to the eldest to lead the Clan as a whole, but each brother had his own bailiwick of responsibility. Five strong Alphas in charge meant the Clan could expand to five times the size of a normal Clan, or even larger. They all knew how to delegate and put trust in their top people.

They also knew when it was wise to make alliances with other strong groups of shifters, and that's why Redstone wasn't just a cougar Clan. It had members from all shifter species under its umbrella and was one of the strongest organizations in the world, not just its native North America.

Stopped at a light on the outskirts of town, Den reached into his zippered jacket pocket and pulled out a tiny earpiece, lifting his helmet briefly to put it in place. He'd been so out of it after that amazing kiss he hadn't thought to do so before he took off.

"Hey, Bri, you read me?" Den asked as he took off again once the light turned green.

"Loud and clear," came the answer at once in his earpiece. "All quiet on the western front."

Brian could be a smartass, but he was a good operative with plenty of military experience. One of the older cats in the Clan, Brian had passed his century mark a few years before but was still a vital member of the Clan. He looked about forty to most humans and would for many years to come. He had been in both World Wars and given up soldiering years ago, but he still knew how to do surveillance. He'd kept his skills sharp and enjoyed the latest in tech gear. He was part of Redstone's security team and was working on the project in town during the day shift. He'd agreed to help Den out at night since the ranch was a bit too large for just one man to watch completely.

Brian was going to watch from the road while Den planned to go past the ward, if he could, and prowl the property from inside in his cougar form. Brian had other men from his security detail that he could call in if there was trouble. Whenever Redstone Construction took on a large project, they always had a team of guys ready to watch over the building site. Brian's night shift was on duty over there right now, in fact, and the neighborhood was only about fifteen minutes away by car. Faster, if one happened to be a shifter and could go on foot or by air.

Brian had told Den that half his security crew this time were flight shifters, so air support was a very real possibility. It might not be fighter jets with missiles, but silent feathered air support was even better, in these circumstances. They had sharp beaks and terrifying claws and could swoop down almost without sound, out of a dark sky. Whether they were hawks, owls or eagles, they were deadly and accurate, day or night, and a shifter bird was usually a hell of a lot larger than their wild counterparts.

"The lady is heading home. I'm on her tail," Den reported to Brian over his headset.

"Roger that. I'm tucked out of sight and set up for the night," Brian reported. "See you when you get here."

CHAPTER 7

The rest of the ride back to the ranch went uneventfully, thank goodness. Den stopped his bike a good distance from where Sunny pulled in, making her way down the long driveway to the ranch house. The area immediately surrounding the house was cleared of trees, but there was a nice forested area not too far distant. That was where Den would be prowling, at first. He wanted to be certain nothing could stalk her from there.

Den rolled his bike the rest of the way with the motor and lights off. He passed the driveway and made his way stealthily to where Brian had parked his dark sedan under some camouflaging trees. If Den hadn't known Brian was there, he never would have spotted him. Den rolled up to Brian's window and took off his helmet.

"Any activity?" Den asked.

"Nothing. The parents are gone, I think. I had Hans on day shift with Luke. Luke didn't see a thing from out here, but Hans did a little aerial recon and left you some notes." Brian handed over a scrap of paper.

Den took a close look at it in the dim light. As a shifter, he didn't need much light to see in the dark. He had the night vision of his animal counterpart and could easily see the little map Hans had drawn of the ranch.

"This is great. I'm going to attempt to cross the ward in my fur and see what I can of the place from the ground. I'll be going in through that grove of trees on the other end of the property. I won't be in radio contact for a while, but if anything big happens, just honk your horn, and I'll hear it," Den instructed.

"Will do," Brian agreed readily. "Good luck out there. I'll keep my ears on for when you're two-legged again. Check in when you're back, okay?"

Den wanted to sigh, but Brian was right. He'd taught all the younger Clansmen about safety in surveillance, so Den couldn't really object. He nodded and rolled on, waiting until he was far enough from the ranch to start up his engine and head for the other end of the ranch property. There was a road back there where he could leave his bike in the trees and approach through that grove, to the backyard and rear of the house. It didn't take long.

Den stripped and put his clothing in his saddlebags, then let his body change into that of his animal spirit. From one moment to the next he went from human to cougar, dropping to all fours and prowling forward. He was on the hunt.

The ward around the property was strong, but it let him through after tickling his fur for a moment. If it was set against evil, it made sense that it would let Den through. He was dedicated to the Light and the Mother of All. He meant no one on this property any harm, and that was probably part of the intent of the ward, lucky for him.

Den prowled closer, noting the scents in the trees. Normal things. Animals, plants, and…magic? He started moving more quickly, breaking into a trot. The scent of magic was fresh, and there was a slight tingle in the air as he moved through it. Something was going on not too far away.

He didn't sense danger. On the contrary, whatever was happening felt…natural. Good, in some way that he couldn't quite define. Curiosity, which was a natural instinct of his inner cat, led him forward through the dense woodland.

The trees here were a bit more crowded than he'd expected. They blocked his view of whatever was in front of him very effectively. As he drew closer, he got little flashes of someone moving in a small clearing that lay ahead. His fur stood on end. Was this an intruder? Someone who wasn't supposed to be on the family's land?

Or had he happened upon something the family wanted to keep hidden? Was someone in the family performing some sort of magical rite out here under the moonlight?

He couldn't see it under the canopy of trees, but Den knew there was a full moon tonight. It sang through his blood. Though he could shape shift at any time of the month, the full moon drew him, as it did most shifters, to let their wild side run free.

Den prowled closer, able to see a figure floating through the trees now. Just little vertical snatches of gauzy white through the columns of tree trunks. The movements were graceful, almost like a dance, and the smell of blooming flowers tickled his nose. The heady aroma of flowers, and something even more alluring to his senses.

Sunny.

Her unique scent came to him on the night air. What in the world was she doing out here in the middle of the woods?

Not that he wasn't glad to see her at any time, day or night, but he was concerned for her safety. If she was all alone out here, who was watching her back? If not for him, no one. That thought made him want to growl, but he held it back. He had to take stock of the entire situation first, to be certain that she was completely alone.

His instincts and senses told him that she was the only being out here besides a few small woodland creatures. Bunnies that scampered out of his way or froze, hoping he wouldn't see them, a family of owls in an old oak tree, and the occasional sleeping nest of squirrels, among others.

As he stalked closer, he could see the moonlight filtering down through the leaves into a clearing. It was a perfect circle. Perhaps, a sacred circle?

Its very existence on this land told him things about the family that lived here. Such things didn't put themselves in the hands of non-magical folk. Such things didn't just sprout up anywhere. Even among those with magic, only a special few were entrusted with places of power like this.

As he made his way through the trees, he could see more. Sunny moved slowly through the sacred circle, as if in a dance. A slow dance that wasn't terribly athletic, but it held a magic all its own. Wherever she moved, plants grew, and flowers blossomed. Night-blooming flowers that were as delicate as she was.

She was creating her very own sylvan glade with the magic of her dance. He cleared the final section of trees and was standing just outside the circle, watching her. Sunny paused and turned to face him.

"Welcome, feline friend," she said, her tone cautious and curious. "I've never seen one of your kind here before, but the trees tell me you will not harm me. I hope they're right." Now, she sounded a bit nervous, and he thought maybe he'd wrecked the peace of her evening by showing himself to her in his furry form.

Den tried to look as innocent as possible. He rubbed up against the tree next to him, doing his best to appear like a harmless house cat. Her wide eyes told him he wasn't succeeding. He had to do something to make it a bit clearer that what he wasn't going to hurt her. Moving slowly, he prowled toward her, proud of her gumption when she didn't move a muscle.

He bumped his head against her hand, and he could feel her breathe a sigh of relief as her fingers stroked over the tawny fur behind his ears. He leaned into her hand and then reached up to lick her fingers.

The taste of her skin nearly undid him. Shifters were all

about their senses. Scent was the easiest to attain, touch was next, but taste was a bit harder. He had kissed her earlier, in his human form, but his senses were so much sharper when he wore his fur.

"You are friendly, aren't you?" Sunny's laugh was charming as she smiled at him. Then, her head tilted as she looked into his eyes. "There's something familiar about you." She paused and considered. "Have we met before?"

He was surprised by her words. It almost sounded as if she knew about shifters.

"One of my dearest friends is a Russian tigress, so if you're that kind of cat, I want you to know you're safe here. All beings of good intent and peaceful hearts are welcome in our woods."

Son of a bitch! She *did* know about shifters. There was currently a very famous prima ballerina who was from a notorious Russian tiger Clan. Den sat back on his haunches and thought about the implications.

This actually made things a lot easier. If she knew about his kind, he could shift in front of her and talk a lot more openly. It was clear she knew at least a bit about her own magic, and it sounded like her parents were some sort of mages. Making a quick decision, Den let the change come over him.

Sunny watched the scary mountain lion with wary eyes. He seemed friendly enough, but she knew big cats could be very dangerous, and she wasn't spry enough to outrun him or fight him off if he chose to take a bite out of her hide. She gathered what little magic she could command and tried to be ready for anything.

Then, he shifted.

She'd only seen her ballerina friend shift once, and it had been memorable. This shift was happening much closer and much faster. One minute, there was a cat next to her. The next, there was a swirl of magic, and then, there was a man. A very naked man.

A man she knew. Sunny gasped. A man she'd had dinner with just an hour or two before.

"Den! What in the world?" She was shocked, to say the least.

"This is why I asked if you knew about magic," Den said, standing in front of her, gloriously naked. He didn't seem to be self-conscious at all.

Of course, with a body like his, he had no need to be self-conscious. He was built like a Greek god. Michelangelo's David had nothing on Den, in the flesh. *Hoo boy.* Was the temperature going up? She felt suddenly hot.

"You're a shifter." Sunny's brain hadn't quite caught up with everything yet.

Den nodded. "And you're an elemental."

"I'm a what-now?" She frowned. She'd never really heard that word before.

Sunny's tiger shifter friend had thought Sunny might be some kind of fairy. Or a witch of some sort. But since the only thing she could really do was make things bloom and talk to trees, they hadn't spoken of it much more than that. Sunny had only seen the other woman shift once, and they'd never really talked about it because that one time had been a mistake.,

Luckily for both of them, Sunny had already known about magic and the existence of shifters, so her friend Irena hadn't gotten in trouble. If Sunny had been a non-magical person, who didn't understand the need for secrecy, things might've gone differently.

"You talk to the forest. You make things grow. You're the descendant of a dryad, Sunny. It's why I was sent here to find you," Den admitted, blowing her mind completely.

"I'm adopted," Sunny replied, unable to really comprehend what he'd just said.

"I know that," Den told her, smiling gently. "I also know that you're descended from a powerful dryad named Leonora, and she has tasked one of her other great-granddaughters to find the others and bring them together."

"Why? And how do they know I'm one of them? I've never had blood family. If they knew about me, why did nobody ever claim me?" Sunny's mind was awhirl with questions.

"Why? Because Leonora was poisoned some time ago and is currently hovering between worlds, her life sustained by a willow tree. She needs a number of her granddaughters to gather and combine their magic in a spell that will release her from the tree and heal her wound. I know you're one of them because part of the dryad magic is to call forth a family tree. I don't know exactly how that works, but the one who sent me was able to find you from the tree. She only just learned how to do it, which is why she never knew about you before. She was raised in foster care, herself, and never knew she had relatives. Just an affinity for growing things. Like you."

"So, they didn't know about me before now?" Sunny asked, just to be certain. It felt surreal to be having this kind of conversation with a naked man she'd just seen transform from a humongous mountain lion.

She was scrupulously not looking any lower than his shoulders. The temptation was there, of course, but she couldn't hold a sensible conversation if she looked lower than that. Den was just too hot to handle, and this was not the time for getting burned. No, this was a moment to seize. To finally learn the truth about her origins. If she could believe him.

Her gut instincts—that had served her well all her life— told her he was on the level. Dear, sweet Mother of All! She actually had blood relatives. The thought boggled her mind.

"They didn't know about you until very recently," Den confirmed. "If they had, they would have sought you out sooner. It was only luck, or perhaps the hand of the Goddess, that brought Leonora into contact with her great-granddaughter. She recognized her power and was able to learn from the great-granddaughter's family tree that she was, indeed, related to Leonora. The branches of that tree contained clues to other descendants, and you were on one of those branches, Sunny. I was sent here to make contact and see if you knew of your heritage." His gaze was kind, his eyes conveying his compassion even as she took in his startling words.

"It wasn't just chance that brought you to the dance studio." She gasped as a terrible thought occurred to her. "You didn't arrange to have the window shot out as a way to get close to me, did you?"

"I would never put you in danger like that," he objected immediately, looking more than a bit insulted. "For the record, you really were shot at, and I still believe you're in danger. Which is why I came out here tonight to check your family's property for myself. I wanted to make sure you were safe."

That was kind of sweet in a creepy way, but Sunny suspected that shifters lived by their own set of rules. She still couldn't quite believe she was having such a long conversation with a naked man. Usually, when she was with a naked guy, they had other things on their minds. Again, she realized, shifters probably had their own standards of behavior.

"Okay. But why all the subterfuge? Couldn't you have just told me you'd come looking for me?"

"First, I had to evaluate whether you knew about the unseen world or not. The need for secrecy among my kind is paramount. I had to get to know you a little and gauge how you might react to learning what I had to tell you. I was going to keep you under surveillance for a day or so before finding a way to approach you, but the sniper changed my plans in a hurry. I'd only just gotten to town and located the studio when he opened fire," Den admitted.

She wasn't sure why she believed him, but she did. That had been one hell of a coincidence, but she had seen stranger things happen in her kooky magical family. Sometimes, things really did seem orchestrated by some divine hand.

"Actually," he went on, "I hadn't expected to reveal myself to you so soon, but seeing you using your magic changed my plans again." One corner of his mouth tilted upward in a devilish grin that reminded her—as if she needed any reminding—how attractive he was. And how *naked* he was. "So," he crossed his arms and leaned casually against the tree right next to him, "you come here often?"

CHAPTER 8

A bubble of laughter rose up from Sunny's throat. Den's parody of the famous pickup line was perfect for the occasion.

"I like to dance for the full moon. It calls to me," she admitted with a little shrug.

"I know what you mean," he replied, smiling that devilish smile once more that made her pulse speed up just the tiniest bit. "Most shifters find the full moon almost irresistible." He looked around at the circle, now festooned with night-blooming flowers. "Were you about done here? I'd be glad to walk you back to the house, if you are."

She looked around and nodded in satisfaction. "I suppose so. It's not how it used to be. Before my accident, I mean. I used to really be able to dance, and the dancing somehow activated my ability to make things bloom and grow. I've learned to compensate a bit, but it's still not quite as easy as I remember it."

"I'm sorry, Sunny. That's got to be hard," he said gently. "Have you looked into any of the magical healing alternatives?"

Den straightened as she began walking slowly out of the circle of trees. He followed her steps, not crowding her, but staying close as she picked her way through the densely packed trees.

"My folks talked about it a bit, but they're not really all that well connected. They're artists that dabble in magic, but they're not very powerful. At least, not in the ways that matter to their families. Their union was not sanctioned, but they were in love and decided to go their own way." She shrugged, knowing her parents had sacrificed a lot to be together, but they were still deeply in love all these years later, so it had definitely been the right course of action.

"Did they put up the ward around the property?" Den asked quietly as they made their way toward the edge of the trees.

"Ward?" Sunny was surprised. She'd heard of wards, but she didn't know they'd built one. "If there is one, I suspect they did. Or maybe one of their guests did it for them. They do still have some friends in their extended families, and they sometimes come to visit. They also have a few magical friends who come here to decompress and dabble in art."

"Art can be magical," Den offered quietly as they walked.

"That's what my parents say." She was pleased by his observation. Most magic users had no time for her parents' chosen form of expression.

Sunny realized she shouldn't have been surprised by Den's perception. Their dinner conversation had proven he was a man of deep thought.

And incredible muscles. She couldn't help but notice, even though she tried not to look too closely. She didn't want to ogle the man. That would be rude. But he certainly was easy on the eyes. *Hubba hubba.*

"Speaking of your parents, where are they? I don't perceive anyone in the house."

They were crossing the backyard and were close to the kitchen door, which she had left unlocked. Nobody ever came out here to trouble them. It was safe enough to leave one of the doors open while she danced under the moon.

"They're away on an art retreat. They had the opportunity to take a master class with someone famous that they admire. Have you heard of Roderigo Cortez?"

Den began to laugh. "Rody is a shifter. A related species. He's one of the jaguars from South America who have recently moved to that island Mark Pepard bought for them all."

"Wait. You mean to say that Mark Pepard, the reclusive billionaire, is a shifter?" She shook her head in disbelief.

"Yeah, that's about the worst kept secret among shifters ever since he got married. The jaguars have a slightly different power structure than the rest of us. Most big cats do, in fact. We cougars more closely identify with the rest of the shifters in North America, and we follow the Lords. Most of the other big cat Clans have different hierarchies. Some of them have monarchs, I hear. The jaguars have several different Clans, each with an Alpha-Beta structure that I don't completely understand. Mark is the Alpha, but his second-in-command is his Beta and security chief. Maybe you've heard about the guy who married that famous movie star, Sullivan Lane. He's the Beta in that Clan. And there are quite a few other famous members, including Rody. They're all showboats, those jaguars." Den chuckled, and Sunny could tell he liked the jaguars despite his words.

"They sound interesting. I wonder what my parents will make of your Roderigo? I don't think they've ever really mixed with shifters before, though they know of their existence. Mom's the one who told me about them when I came into my power," Sunny admitted, reaching for the kitchen door. "Would you like to come in?"

What was she doing, inviting him inside her house? Her *empty* house. Where anything could happen because they were the only two people on the property. *Oh, my.*

She went into the kitchen, and he followed, looking around as she headed for the sink. She needed a glass of water. Suddenly, her mouth was completely dry.

"Would you like some water or juice or something? The bathroom is just through there. You can get a towel, if you'd like to...uh...cover up." Blushing furiously, she busied herself with the sink while Den prowled into the bathroom. She felt like a ninny, but she wasn't used to having a naked man walking around in the house.

Den came back with one of the cheery yellow bath towels wrapped around his hips. Oh, boy. He looked even better this way, if such a thing was possible. She hadn't let herself look too much before, but now... All bets were off now.

She could look to her heart's content at those washboard abs that had nothing to do with a gym and everything to do with being an animal on the inside. The thought fired her senses as she wondered what he'd be like in bed. Would his wild side come out to play, and if so, in what ways? She was dangerously close to throwing caution to the wind in her need to find out.

She sipped her water as he moved back into the kitchen and walked up to her. She was frozen in place, her back to the countertop beside the sink, leaning against it. What was he doing?

"Water sounds good," he told her as he took the half-empty glass from her hands and downed the rest of it in a few sexy, slow-motion gulps. Oh, brother, she was in trouble.

He moved away after placing the glass in the sink. Den sauntered over to the kitchen table and leaned one hip against one of the high-backed chairs, facing her.

"So, how long are your folks gone for?" Den asked. His tone was casual, but his golden eyes zeroed in on her like lasers. Magic swirled deep within them, if she wasn't much mistaken.

"Just until Monday," she replied. It was Friday today, so she'd be on her own the whole weekend. "This is the first time they've left me on my own since the accident, so I expect Mom to call every few hours. I spoke to her just before I went outside, in fact. She worries."

"Sounds like a good mom," Den commented, nodding with approval.

"She is, but since moving back in here, I've felt like I was going backward a bit. I went from being a world traveler, woman on her own, to being a kid again, living in my parents' house. In my old room, in fact." She chuckled, despite the intimacy of the situation.

Only the small light above the kitchen table gave off an orange and red glow through its stained-glass shade. The light was on a timer and would stay on until dawn, lighting the way should anyone wake up in the middle of the night and want a snack or something to drink.

"Is it pink?" Den asked, that devilish smile back on his handsome face.

"What? My room? No. It's better," she confided with a teasing lift of her eyebrows. "It's purple. Light purple. A shade called Lilac Breeze. I picked it out all by myself when I was ten."

He laughed along with her. "Sounds perfect," he told her. "I'd love to see it."

Had he really just said that? *Oh, wow.* Her stomach was down by her toes somewhere, the bottom having dropped out of it when his tone had gone all husky and low. Sexuality personified. That's what he was. Dangerous for any woman's sanity.

Den moved, prowling closer, and Sunny couldn't find it within herself to stop him. She knew she could. Just a word and he'd leave her be, but she didn't want the night to end. She wanted to know what it would be like to be with him.

There was something so compelling... So...important...about him.

Like he was essential to her existence, in some way she couldn't yet define. All she knew was that for right now, she wanted to spend the rest of the night being with him.

It had been so long since she'd had a lover. Not since before her accident. Somehow, the male dancer she'd been serious with paled in comparison to Den's svelte muscles and gliding stalk. There was something so primal about him. He stirred every last one of her senses. Her mind, included. She'd greatly enjoyed their banter over dinner. He'd been witty and intelligent in a way that had sparked her admiration and desire.

She only wished she was the woman she used to be, with a body undamaged by crumpled metal and months of hospital care. She wished she could match him in athleticism, but she knew those days were long gone. She was lucky she could even walk right now. That had been in question for months.

He was right in front of her, his height imposing, but not threatening in any way. He was gentle for such a big man. He'd proven that already in their first encounter. It had only been a quick kiss in the dark outside the restaurant, but she'd felt weak in the knees and not from her injuries. She'd wanted more, but it had been impossible right then. Now? All bets were off. They were alone in the house, and there was nothing and no one to stop them from going all the way.

She made a decision and stepped into his arms, closing that final short distance between them. His lips were on hers, their breathing increasing as desire rose.

"You drive me wild, Sunny," he murmured against her lips. "Will you let me drive you wild too?"

"You already do," she admitted, loving the way his lips teased hers.

It was a sexy move she'd never experienced before. Her former lover had been very fast to the mark, so to speak, and hadn't spent a lot of time on seduction. Den, however, seemed to be all about the play, like the cat that shared his soul. She sensed she was in for a treat. No way would she turn this man out into the cold. Not anytime soon, at least.

She kissed him, this time, merging their lips as she wrapped her arms around his neck and pressed against his hard muscled chest. He wore only the towel, and she was wearing her nightdress. She felt his hands at her thighs, lifting the sheer cotton fabric a little at a time. It was agony. It was ecstasy. Or it would be, soon enough.

Their tongues dueled, bringing increasing pleasure as Den scooped her up onto the kitchen counter, his hands on her butt. She gasped as the cold of the stone countertop bled through the thin cotton of her nightgown. Den spread her thighs and stepped between. She didn't have any underwear on under the nightdress, which was hiked up to the tops of her thighs.

She felt on fire with need in a way she had never experienced before. No man had ever sent her senses soaring so high, so fast. No other lover had ever made her feel so much with just the slightest touch.

Not that she'd had many men. Just a few, over the years. Relationships she'd thought would lead to something permanent, but somehow never had. She'd gone into each relationship with such high hopes, only to have them dashed when time and circumstance drew them apart.

This time, she hoped, she was going in with her eyes open. She wasn't the young dreamer any longer. She was a woman who had been through hell in the past year. She'd lost her livelihood and her *raison d'etre*, but she was still alive. Still walking, even if she didn't manage that very well sometimes. She would take Den as her lover, but she wouldn't expect anything more. How could she? He was a shifter. There were probably some kind of rules about who shifters could marry. He would probably settle down with a nice little shifter wife someday.

But, for now, he was all hers, and she intended to make the most of the experience.

CHAPTER 9

Sunny felt Den move closer, spreading her thighs even farther apart. He still had the towel wrapped around his hips, but that was no impediment. She would have him, and she would have him soon. Her mind raced with the wonder of that thought. She felt so free with him. So able to be herself and express her desires. She'd never really felt like this before.

"Tell me you want this," Den whispered against her neck, placing little nibbling kisses down her throat that lit her world on fire.

"I want it. I want *you*," she agreed wholeheartedly. "Don't make me wait."

Den made a rumbling sound of approval as he nosed his way into the neckline of her flimsy nightdress to kiss the swells of her breasts. The neckline was elastic, and it didn't take much for him to pull it downward and reveal her aching peaks. He kissed his way across her body, pausing to suck and lave with his talented tongue while she sighed and moaned with delight.

She squirmed to get closer to him, inching toward the

edge of the countertop and spreading her thighs wide. He seemed to understand what she wanted, moving his hands to her thighs and inching up the fabric that still covered them mid-way. As she moved closer to him, he slid the fabric upward, revealing more and more of her skin, and that secret place that ached for his possession.

She ran her hands down his muscular chest, enjoying the hard ripples of his mid-section, and then lower. The towel was a hindrance, so she slipped the end he'd tucked in the front free and pushed it away. She tried to reach for him, but he trapped her hands with his and met her gaze.

"You do that, this'll end way too soon, princess," he warned, his smile devilish once again. How she loved that particular expression on his handsome face.

"Then, give me what I want," she dared him.

"Are you sure?" His tone was teasing, his eyes lit with a fire of desire that sparked her own.

She nodded slowly. "Very sure."

He growled. Just a little, but definitely a growl. Sweet heaven! That was sexy.

Den placed her hands on his shoulders, then put one hand between them and one on her lower back, guiding her gently forward as he held himself ready for entry. She complied, moving closer at his urging, going slow as he controlled her with his gentle but firm touch on her butt. His hands were so strong. His manner was so masterful. This was no callow boy, but a man who knew exactly what he wanted and precisely how to get it.

Everything about him turned her on. She was breathless by the time she felt the first touch of that velvety head against her inner core. He invaded by slow increments, allowing her to get used to him. The feel, the girth, the length. He was more than she'd ever had before, and she finally understood a little bit of the things her friends would giggle about and whisper over when they talked of their lovers and their various attributes.

Bigger definitely was better. At least in this instance. He

filled her completely, leaving no part of her untouched or uninfluenced by his presence. She was complete. Possessed utterly...and ready to find out what pleasure he could ultimately bring her. She only hoped she could keep her sanity after this encounter. So far, he was damn close to blowing her mind, and they hadn't really even started yet.

Den began to move, slowly at first then more swiftly as things started to heat up. She clung to him, depending on him to keep her safely perched on the edge of the countertop, trapped between it and his hard body. His arms were around her, supporting her, molding her to him and making her feel protected and cared for in a way she hadn't expected. At one point, he buried his head in the curve of her neck, and she felt his teeth and tongue teasing the sensitive area.

His pace increased again and again until he was making short, fast, hard strokes that drove her absolutely wild with want. She could feel the crisis coming and almost feared its intensity. Den pressed her close against his chest, and she felt a rumbling vibration against her breasts that was the last straw. She climaxed with a gasp, biting her lip to keep from crying out at the amazing feelings coursing through her body.

Den came a moment later with a growl that sounded almost like the cougar that shared his soul and a clenching of his muscles that kept her pressed hard against him in every way. She might have blacked out for a few seconds. She couldn't be sure, but regardless, she knew this encounter with Den had been the most intense pleasure of her life. Nothing and no one could match it.

It was a long time before either of them moved. Finally, Den shifted a little, releasing the pressure of his hold, which she hadn't really minded at all. She'd liked the way he'd clung to her and allowed her to do the same.

"Are you okay, princess?"

His voice was rough with passion fulfilled, and the look in his eyes melted her heart. It looked like he truly cared about her condition. The few men she'd been with before Den hadn't ever looked at her that way. Heck, after the act was over, they'd barely looked at her at all, preferring to roll over and go to sleep.

She really liked the way he called her *princess* too. That was new. No man had ever given her a pet name like that before. It made her feel special.

"I'm fantastic," she told him with complete candor. "How about you?"

The grin that stretched his lips made her tingle in a good way.

"Never better," he said, emphasizing the first word.

She smiled back at him then yelped as he gathered her into his arms and lifted her off the counter. She wrapped her legs around his waist when it became clear he wasn't going to let her go, and he walked slowly out of the kitchen and down the hall. He zeroed in on her lilac-walled bedroom and carried her inside. She usually left her bedroom door open, so it hadn't been hard for him to locate.

Den deposited her on her bed and stood above for a moment, gazing down at her. She felt her temperature rise with desire and noticed something else rising, also. She licked her lips, and he growled.

"Are you ready for more, princess?" he asked, the growl clear in his voice in a way that made her squirm with eagerness.

In answer, she held out her arms, and he stalked onto the bed, joining her. It was barely big enough for the both of them, but it would do.

They made love again, then again, and finally fell into sleep sometime deep in the night.

*

"Movement on the perimeter." Brian's disembodied voice sounded in the earpiece Den had put back in as a precaution when he'd retrieved his clothes earlier. "Doesn't look friendly."

Den was instantly awake. Much as he would like to laze around in Sunny's bed a little longer, if there was trouble, they had to be ready. He was out of the bed and getting dressed, making a little noise on purpose so that Sunny would also wake. When he looked over at her, she was blinking at him.

"We have to get up, princess. There may be some trouble heading this way, and I want you well clear of it before it can get to you." He paused for a moment to lean in and give her a kiss. He wanted more, but there was no time. "Get dressed. Put on something warm. My motorcycle is stashed in the woods. We'll head for that."

Eyes wide as she started to understand the situation, Sunny scrambled out of the bed and headed for the bathroom.

"How do you know?" she asked, looking at him over her shoulder as she passed by. He was seated on the edge of the bed, leaning over to put on his boots.

He was glad he'd taken the time to retrieve his clothing. Preparation and attention to detail had always stood him well in the past. They were doing so now, again.

Den finished with his boots and stood. Sunny came out of the bathroom and headed for the closet while he answered her question.

"I've got some help outside, watching the house. There's an operative parked down the road from your mailbox. He just radioed me." He pointed toward his ear. "I've got a tiny tactical radio that we use for this kind of thing. Luckily, I remembered to put it back in my ear when I came back with my clothes."

"That's…pretty cool, actually," she said finally as she dressed in haste. When she reached for a white top, he stopped her.

"Dark colors, princess. Black, brown, dark blue or green. We want to blend in to the night and the forest."

She gulped and nodded, reaching for a different hangar with a sleek black top instead of the white one. It had long sleeves. He nodded, pleased with her quick understanding of the situation.

She was ready as quickly as he could have wished. He grabbed his stuff and headed into the kitchen. The house was going to be empty all weekend, so he took stock of anything that might need to be put away. She joined him a moment later.

"Do you trust me?" he asked, meeting her gaze, knowing her answer was vital. He had to have her trust in order to make this work.

She nodded. "I do, but I can't explain exactly why. Especially when you're scaring the heck out of me right now." A nervous laugh escaped her, and he knew he had to calm her somehow. At least a little.

"I'm sorry. I know this is all very abrupt. Thing is, if you're in danger, the best place to be is somewhere safe. If the bad guys have tracked you to your home, I don't really want you to be out here all alone all weekend. It could be that your parents' presence kept the attackers at bay, but your folks aren't here right now, and you're vulnerable. I can fix that, but you'll need to trust me."

"How can you fix it?" she asked in a small voice.

"By taking you someplace else for the weekend," he replied immediately. There was no doubt in him. He wanted her away from here. With him. Safe.

She gulped visibly. Then, she looked around as if lost for a single moment. His heart sank, but she straightened her spine and met his gaze once more.

"Where will we go?"

Sweet Mother of All. She was going to go for it. He sent a silent prayer of thanks up to the Lady and refocused on the matter at hand.

"Well, first, I'm taking you to the construction site where my Clanmates are working. They're living in some of the houses as they work on the others. There's plenty of room. In fact, that's where I'm staying. And with all of them around, I dare anyone of ill intent to try to get to you there. We can stay there for the rest of the night, but in the morning, I'd like you to consider going to Wyoming with me so you can meet your relative. I have access to a private plane, and I can have you there and back before your parents return, if that's your wish. I'd just like you to meet her and hear what she has to say. It'll also be much safer for you there than anywhere else, and relocating, even briefly, might just throw your enemies off your trail for a while." He realized he was pushing very hard, so he backed off a tiny bit. "Just think about it. We can stay with the Clan all weekend, if you prefer to stay in town. You don't have to decide right away. For now, we just need to get out of here and get you to safety. Is there anything you'll need from here?"

Her head lifted, and she looked around. "Give me a minute." She left the kitchen and headed back into the house at a fast pace.

Den used the time to contact Brian and get a sit rep. The report wasn't good, though Brian was doing a good job gathering intel on the people who were doing their best to break the ward around the property. Brian had called for backup, but it would take a while to get here. Den advised Brian of his plan to bug out and suggested he cancel the cavalry and get going himself once Den and Sunny were clear. Brian agreed with the strategy and confirmed he would keep watch until he heard from Den, then head back to Clan territory, following Den's path and acting as rear guard.

Den was glad to have Brian on the case. There was no one better to watch Den's back and help him keep Sunny safe. She walked back into the kitchen with a small nylon computer bag slung across her body.

"If I'm going to be gone for a couple of days, I'll need my laptop so my folks can call. They like to video chat every night."

Den just nodded and led the way to the kitchen door. He opened it just as the night sky lit with a red-orange glow. Fire?

"Be advised. They're lobbing fireballs at the ward," Brian said calmly in Den's ear. "Looking for weak spots, I'd say, and it looks like they just found one by the driveway. You'd better get moving. It won't take them long to exploit the crack in the ward."

"We're on our way out the back door," Den replied over the radio, then looked at Sunny. "We've got to move," he told her. "My backup reports there's a weakness in the ward, and the bad guys are trying to break through."

"I don't really know what that all means, but I'm trusting you, Den," she told him, grabbing his forearm and meeting his gaze. "Don't ever make me regret it."

"Never," he answered solemnly, then lowered his head to seal his vow with a kiss. Not a very long kiss. They didn't have time for what he really wanted, but he had to kiss her. To reassure her and himself that this—this thing between them—was worth fighting for. When he ended the kiss, he smiled at her. "I'm going to have to fill you in on a few things regarding the use of magic, but for now, just trust me. We do not want to meet these people head on. Our best chance at this point is to bug out."

"Then, what are we waiting for?"

Sunny exited the back door before he could stop her. Den had to admire her gumption, but he could've wished she'd wait for him to check things before she dove in headfirst. Still, they were on the move, which was ultimately a good thing.

They retraced their earlier steps, heading toward the trees at the back of the property. When the sky overhead flashed red, Sunny gasped and clutched her chest.

"What was that?" she asked in a scared whisper.

"Nothing good," Den muttered as he encouraged her to keep walking. "The folks trying to get in have a mage lobbing magical energy at your ward, trying to break it down."

"So, they can't come onto the property until they break it?" she asked. "But then, how did you get here?"

"Your ward is set to keep evil out. I'm not evil, so it let me through." He shrugged as they kept moving. He wished they could move faster, but she had limitations from her injuries.

She didn't say anything more as they went along. He knew

she was moving as quickly as she could, but it wasn't fast enough. Then, she stumbled on something, and he reached out and scooped her into his arms, breaking into a lope as the sky above them turned red again.

"You don't have to carry me," she protested, but looped her arms around his neck.

"I don't mind. I like having you in my arms," he told her, sparing a moment to smile down at her despite the danger they were in.

"Can other people see that?" she asked nervously as the sky turned red again.

"Only those with magic," he assured her.

They were in the trees now, heading for Den's bike.

"The trees don't like the red light," she said suddenly. "They're warning me to flee."

"Smart trees."

CHAPTER 10

Sunny couldn't believe she was being carried along at a running pace. It was embarrassing to be so dependent on him, but by the same token, it was amazing to experience the true strength of the man. He wasn't even breathing hard, and she wasn't exactly light as a feather. Sure, she was slim, but even the male dancers she'd known wouldn't have been able to carry her like this while running such a long distance. Den, once again, was proving to be something extraordinary.

Once they were in the trees, she opened her senses and listened. They were clearly upset and worried for her safety. They were telling her to leave. To run fast and far. It was good to have their confirmation of the peril. Not that she didn't believe Den, but she was cautious by nature.

She'd only known Den a short time, after all.

He began to slow and then put her down. He continued walking just a short distance, and there, behind a tree, hidden in the darkness of the undergrowth, was a sleek black motorcycle. Den rolled it out of the bushes and into the open.

He reached down and retrieved a helmet, handing it to her. She took it and looked at him.

"What about you?" she asked.

"I've only got the one with me, and I'd rather you wore it, both for safety, and because it'll help disguise you a bit more," he explained.

Sunny understood his point and put on the black helmet. It fit reasonably well, if just a tiny bit large, but it would do. Den got on the monster of a bike, and she climbed aboard behind him, even as the sky glowed red again. She could just see it through the trees, and forest was not only afraid for her but angry at those who were trying to intrude on her family's property.

"We're on our way," Den said, and she realized he was talking to the man on the other end of his radio. She couldn't hear the reply, but Den agreed to rendezvous with the other man at the construction site then thanked him. He did all this while rolling the bike toward the roadway that ran behind her parents' property.

When they were on the pavement, he started the bike and reached behind to grab her hands and tuck them snuggly around his waist under his leather jacket. She liked the feel of his warmth and his hard muscles under the soft T-shirt. Everything about him stirred her senses. Now that she knew the delight that could be had with him, she thought for sure she would be spoiled for anyone else. But she'd deal with that when the time came. For now, she was going to enjoy her time with this most amazing man.

They were zipping down the road behind her parents' property when the sky lit with a bright red glow that lasted a bit longer than the others. She tried to listen to the trees and got the impression of the dome of protection, which she had been unaware of until Den had told her about it, falling. Breaking. Cracking to allow bad things inside. The dome had held the evil at bay, but it was gone now, and bad things— and beings—were entering the once protected area.

Sunny shuddered. Her parents were going to be very

upset. They would have been even more upset had she not escaped. If not for Den, she would've been unaware. A sitting duck for whatever those people had in mind.

At least with Den, she felt safe. She had the overwhelming sense that he would take care of her. He would protect her and do everything in his power to make sure that she didn't fall into the hands of the wrong people. She trusted him. More than that, she was more than halfway in love with him, if she was being honest with herself.

But that would never do. He was a shapeshifter. There were probably strict rules about who they could associate with on a permanent basis. And besides, who would want to deal with her limitations on an ongoing basis? That question had bothered her ever since the accident, when her dancer boyfriend had deserted her. She couldn't dance. She could barely walk properly. What able-bodied man would want to tie himself to someone like her?

Depression had been her near-constant companion for a long time. She had done everything she could to try to work her way out of it, but every now and then, it still came to call.

Just then, they hit the main road, and Den let the motorcycle fly. She held onto him for dear life, exhilarated by the ride. She'd never been on a motorcycle before, but she decided she loved the sensation. Maybe, after all of this was over, she would get one. Not as big or ferocious as this one, but something fun and fast and more her size.

Sunny knew where they were going. They were headed to that section of town where the big old houses were that Redstone Construction was renovating. There were several in a small area, and they were all in various stages of completion. They'd been the talk of the town for a while now as the old homes were restored to their former glory.

Den whisked her along through the pre-dawn traffic at a high rate of speed. It probably wasn't legal for him to not be wearing a helmet, but they didn't run afoul of any police as he drove them steadily toward Midtown. When they arrived in front of a gorgeous Victorian house that had been restored, there was a big man on the porch, waiting for them. He came down the steps and met them as Den parked the bike.

"Brian followed me in," Den said without preamble as he climbed off the bike after Sunny. "Jer, this is Sunny. Sunny, my brother-in-law, Jerry."

"Nice to meet you." Sunny nodded at the big man as she took off the helmet.

"Likewise," Jerry replied then shook hands with Den. "I'll take the bike around back. You go on in."

"Thanks, Jer. I'll see you inside."

Den put his hand at the small of Sunny's back and guided her up the steps into the old Victorian. She couldn't wait to see inside. The exterior was gorgeous, and she'd always wanted to know what these places looked like on the interior.

"Wow." That's the only word she could utter, at first, as she took in the restored grandeur of the entrance hall. It was lovely inside, just as she'd suspected. "This is beautiful."

She looked up at the ceiling and admired the small chandelier that lit the way. The woodwork all around was gleaming and intricate. Everything had been restored to as close to the original period as possible.

A woman came down the staircase and smiled at them. "It's a little early, even for you, Den," she groused good-naturedly. She stepped right up to Den and kissed his cheek in greeting.

"Couldn't be helped," he replied, returning the gorgeous blonde's kiss, then turned to Sunny. "This is Sunny," he told the woman. "Sunny, this is my sister, Diane."

The green-eyed monster of jealousy went back to sleep. She was his sister, not some gorgeous girlfriend.

"Pleased to meet you, Diane," Sunny said, reaching forward to shake the woman's hand.

"Likewise," she replied. "I'll show you to your room, and you can decide what to do from there. It's almost dawn, so you might want to stay up and have breakfast. On the other hand, you might want to go back to sleep." Diane spoke as she led the way up the stairs and down the hallway.

"I'm not really sure I could sleep right now," Sunny revealed. "Is it possible I could make some coffee?"

Diane smiled at her. "I see we have a love of caffeine in common. Let me show you the kitchen. There's always a pot of coffee on the go, pretty much any time of day."

Sunny spent the next half hour chatting with Diane over an exceedingly good cup of coffee. Den had gone off somewhere after grabbing mugs of coffee for himself and for Jerry. Another man came into the kitchen, nodded to them, and grabbed a cup of coffee before leaving as silently as he'd entered.

"That's Brian," Diane informed her. "He's been a mentor to Den over the years, and I think he was helping him watch your place."

"I still can't believe what happened out there," Sunny said, feeling very comfortable with Diane. She was the kind of woman who invited confidences and was easy to talk to. "I've never really seen anything like that red fire in the sky. I hope the house is okay."

"I'm sure it will be. If anything was damaged, our guys can fix it for you," Diane offered.

The thought of having a Redstone Construction work crew on call boggled Sunny's mind a little bit. She wondered how her parents would feel about it. She wouldn't do anything without their approval. After all, the ranch was their safe haven. She wouldn't invite anybody else there without their knowledge.

Den's invasion of her home territory didn't really count. The trees had welcomed him. In her mind, somehow, that made it all right. And he was just one person, there to see her, not to meddle with the house or grounds. Her folks were very particular about everything on their property. She wouldn't have someone they didn't know out there to change things, even if it was just a repair stuff. Better to wait until they returned and get their opinion and blessing.

"My mate is the foreman of this work crew. In fact, Jer's in charge of the entire project here in Sacramento. It's been a great experience." Diane gestured to the beautifully refinished kitchen. "I've been really enjoying living in this old house and helping them fix up the others. I do some of the interior design and a little bit of the gardening and landscape design, though that's not really my forte."

"Gardening and the outdoors are sort of my thing," Sunny revealed. "Since my accident, I've really taken to working outside with the flowers and trees. They make me feel whole."

"It was a car accident, wasn't it?" Diane's eyes held both concern and compassion.

"Yes," Sunny nodded as she took a sip of coffee. "Almost a year ago."

"I suppose you've only had human medical intervention, huh?" Diane waited for Sunny to nod agreement before continuing. "Maybe you should look into some magical healing. We shifters have our own internal magic that heals most wounds, but there are healers among us. Priestesses and shamans. People who have the ability to heal others magically. I bet someone like that could help you." Diane shrugged. "It's at least worth looking into. I hope you don't mind me butting my nose in, but the strain on your face tells me that you're in a lot more pain than you let on. Maybe somebody can help you with that. If Den doesn't hook you up with some contacts in that area, let me know, and I'll find someone you can talk to."

"That's...really kind of you. Thanks," Sunny replied, stunned at how open and giving this woman she had only just met was being. Diane had a good soul. That much was clear.

"Sorry," Diane surprised her by saying as she shook her head and smiled. "I've got a lot of maternal instincts, and I tend to mother everybody in the Clan. Feel free to tell me if I'm coming on too strong. I just like to help people."

"I think it's wonderful. Don't apologize," Sunny told her, reaching across the table to pat Diane's hand in a friendly way. "I'm a big believer in following your instincts. If your instinct is to be helpful and kind, I'm sure there are much worse things in the world." Sunny chuckled, and Diane joined in.

That's how Den found them, both laughing and looking relaxed. He breathed an internal sigh of relief. He hadn't been sure how his sometimes-finicky sister would deal with a woman who didn't really understand her role in the magical world. Sunny wasn't a shifter, after all. Den wasn't sure how much contact Diane had with non-shifters these days. To his surprise, they seem to be getting along like old friends.

"Denny!" His sister spotted him before Sunny did and leapt to her feet, rushing over to give him a hug in greeting, even though she'd done so when he'd arrived. Diane was like that. Free with the hugs and generous with her affection toward her family. "She's great," Diane whispered in his ear just before letting him go.

Better and better. Diane really liked Sunny, or she wouldn't have said anything. That was important, because he truly believed Sunny was going to be part of his life for a very long time. Forever, in fact.

"Glad to see you two getting along," he said to both of them when Diane let go.

Diane remained standing and headed for the refrigerator. "It's almost time to start breakfast. Do you two want to help or are you going to try to get more sleep?"

"We can stay for breakfast, but if Sunny agrees, I think we're heading out right after," Den told his sister, looking at Sunny for agreement.

"Where to?" Diane asked before Sunny could say anything. "Back home or to the Wraiths?"

"Wraiths?" Sunny's brows drew together in a concerned frown.

"My brother wants to join an elite military unit made up of ex-Special Forces soldiers, like himself. Only they're mostly werewolves, and they live on a mountaintop in Wyoming," Diane told Sunny before he could say anything. "They're known as the Wraiths because they're scary good at their jobs, and I will admit, they only fight on the side of the Light, which is more than can be said for most mercenaries." Diane wasn't subtle about her disapproval of his plan to join the Wraiths. "We have a perfectly good Clan in Las Vegas with work all over the place, if all you want is travel."

It was an old argument. One she had been repeating over and over ever since he'd revealed his desire to leave the Clan for a spot in the Wraiths. What she didn't yet know was how finding Sunny had changed his future plans. He wasn't sure what he was going to do now. It all depended on what Sunny wanted. He'd do anything to make her happy. He just needed time—and the right moment—to discuss the future with her first, so he could figure out how best to do that.

Den didn't want to move too fast and scare Sunny off. He had to be careful how he presented his desire to keep her in his life forever. She wasn't a shifter. She might not understand the whole concept of fated mates. He would have to go slow and see if she was receptive and then spring it on her a little at a time, if he could.

"You said the dryad and my supposed family is in Wyoming," Sunny said, her tone a bit accusatory. Den winced inwardly.

"The one tasked with finding the rest of the extended family is mated to the leader of the wolf Pack that lives there. The Alpha, Jason, is the younger brother of the leader of the Wraiths, Jesse. Jason leads the entire Pack. Jesse leads the ex-military that have gathered around him," Den explained. "Jesse is mated to another of the dryad's descendants. Another member of your extended family tree. And the dryad, Leonora, has been living on Pack lands for a long time. She's there, as well, though gravely injured at the moment and suspended between worlds in the heart of a willow tree, as I understand it."

"It all sounds incredible," Sunny whispered.

"Yet, I've seen what you can do with plants, and the trees speak to you," Den reminded her. "I have no doubt the information is correct, and you are one of Leonora's descendants. The question is, do you want to meet the others?"

Sunny smiled shakily at him. "I believe I do," she admitted. "I guess that means we'll be going to Wyoming after breakfast." Sunny turned to look at Diane. "What can I do to help?"

"You can keep him from joining the Wraiths," Diane muttered immediately, then shook her head. "You can beat the eggs," she said in a more normal voice, letting the matter of the Wraiths drop, finally, much to Den's relief.

CHAPTER 11

They shared a hearty breakfast with the members of the construction crew. The men ate a mountain of eggs, bacon, sausage, toast and hashbrowns, then took off after cleaning the kitchen, heading out for their various job sites. Sunny learned they were all living in this house—what they were calling the Pack house—for the duration of the project, and most of the men were werewolves, though Jerry told her he was a grizzly bear, and of course, Diane and Den were both cougar shifters.

Sunny was enchanted by it all. The crew seemed to function like a big, boisterous extended family. Something she'd never really had. They included her and teased her, just as they teased each other with good-natured humor. They all made a point to thank her for helping to make their breakfast and insisted on cleaning up.

Well-mannered as well as good company, Sunny felt she could be friends with these people easily. They all seemed to respect Den and especially Jerry and Brian. Sunny had thanked Brian for his part in her escape from the ranch. He'd brushed off her thanks easily but seemed pleased by her words, though he tried not to let it show. Some folks were like that. They didn't take praise or thanks very well, but she felt it was important to give it. Perhaps especially for those who didn't usually hear such things.

Brian was the one who drove Sunny and Den out to a small private airstrip on the outskirts of town an hour later. He waited until they were airborne in the small jet that had been waiting for them before driving away. Sunny could see Brian's truck wheeling away as they took off, Den at the controls of the fancy private jet.

Sunny had never been in the cockpit of a plane before. She'd never flown on something this small or this luxurious either. It was a Redstone Construction jet, with a discreet company logo on the side. The interior was configured for passengers, but with wide, comfy seats that had plenty of space between them. Den had headed for the cockpit, and he'd given her the choice of sitting up there with him or stretching out in back. The seats reclined nearly flat, he'd told her, if she wanted to catch up on the sleep she'd missed earlier.

But she was still a little too wired from all that had happened to be able to sleep. She liked flying and really enjoyed the view from the cockpit as they gained altitude. The fact that Den was a pilot had surprised her at first. Of course, if he'd really been a Special Forces soldier, she'd bet he had a lot of interesting skills she had yet to discover.

"How are you doing over there?" Den asked, looking over at Sunny as the jet started to level out. He'd been talking in what sounded like code over the radio as they gained altitude then made a final transmission and turned to her.

"I'm okay," she replied, smiling. "It's really beautiful up here." She gestured toward the incredible view out the cockpit window.

"I totally agree with you. Best view in the world." Den looked around with satisfaction at the cloud formations they could see out the window. "One of the best perks of learning how to fly."

"When did you?"

"In the service," he told her. "I only recently retired. I was, as my sister told you, a Green Beret. Part of a special unit of other shifters utilized only in very special circumstances."

"I had no idea the military knew about you guys."

"They do, and they don't. We only answer to one particular admiral who's in charge of all of the troops that have some sort of magical ability. He knows about us. He's one of us. But aside from him, I doubt anybody else really knows. Some might suspect, but nobody knows for sure. And that's the way we like it."

"That admiral must be some kind of wizard," she mused.

"Actually, the rumor is he some kind of elemental power. It makes sense. Nobody else could really command respect from the rest of us the way he does. And he's strong enough—or perhaps he has enough dirt on everyone in higher command—that he always gets what he wants. He doesn't deploy the magical troops in any sort of situation that would compromise our allegiance to the Lady's Light."

"You mean the Goddess, right? My family calls her the Mother of all, Gaia, or Mother Earth," Sunny revealed.

"Yeah, it's all pretty much the same. The force of good in the universe," he confirmed. "Our calling is to defeat evil wherever we find it."

"It's a noble calling," Sunny agreed.

Den shrugged, changing the subject. "If you get hungry, there's food and drinks in the back."

"Is that your way of saying that you're hungry?" she teased.

"Well, I could be convinced to eat something." His smile told her she hadn't been far off the mark.

"Are shapeshifters always hungry?" Sunny chuckled as she unbuckled her seatbelt and stood, climbing between the seats in the cramped cockpit.

"Not always, but usually," he replied with a grin as she went into the back of the plane. They had left the door to the cockpit wide open, so they could talk back and forth. Sunny found the small service area which contained a little refrigerator. She opened it and found a supply of sandwiches and other items.

"Which would you rather have?" She shouted to be heard over the noise of the engines. "Turkey on wheat or roast beef on rye?"

"Bring them both up here," he called back. "And some drinks. Juice and water, if it's there."

Damn. She had never seen people eat as much as those shifters this morning. Yet, they were all in top physical condition. They must have amazingly fast metabolisms.

Sunny took one of the plastic bags out of the refrigerator and repacked it with the two sandwiches for Den and one for herself, plus a few drinks. She made sure to include napkins and straws and then headed back toward the cockpit.

They ate, enjoying the view and sharing conversation about their past experiences. Den told her about his life in the Army and how he had decided to retire.

"The thing is, I thought I was ready to work in the construction business, but I've been feeling that something was missing. I petitioned Jesse to join the Wraiths, and you know how my sister feels about that." He rolled his eyes, and Sunny nodded as she nibbled on her sandwich. "It seemed the right step to take at the time, but now, I'm not so sure. It would be hard to break ties with my home Clan and join what is essentially a wolf Pack, but it wouldn't be so bad. I know many of the guys from the service, and we always got along even though I'm a cat and they're a bunch of dogs." He chuckled as he rolled up the paper from his first sandwich and placed it back in the bag.

"So, what has you rethinking your decision?" Sunny had just finished the first half of her own sandwich while he was opening up his second.

The question caught Den by surprise. How much should he reveal? That was a tough one. He'd already decided he didn't want to scare her away, but he should say something to at least see if she was even close to the same thinking that was running through his mind.

"Well, you, for one." He tried to be cool as he evaluated her response. She seemed confused. He needed to say more. To make it clearer. "I never expected to meet you, Sunny, but now that I have, I need to rethink a few things. I'd like to see where our relationship goes. That is, if you feel the same." Now, she looked stunned. He wasn't sure what to think. He hated it, but he had to ask. "Do you want to spend more time with me?"

"I—" She swallowed hard before going on, setting his nerves on edge. "I'd like that," she said finally, and he could breathe again. Satisfaction spread through his body, along with relief. Except, she looked a little embarrassed, and he wasn't sure what to think about that.

"I want you to know. This... What happened between us... It's not a casual thing for me. I hope that doesn't put you off." He was laying it on the line, but his instincts were pushing him onward, even though he knew pressing his luck probably wasn't to his best advantage right now. He'd thought he wasn't going to rush her, but his inner cat had other ideas.

"It doesn't," she answered in a small voice, but he still heard it, and his heart leapt with joy. "I mean... I never thought... After my accident, I didn't think anyone would be interested in anything long-lasting with me."

He turned to look at her, shocked. "Are you kidding me?" The vulnerable look on her face was answer enough for him, and he felt angry on her behalf. "You're the most desirable, decent, intelligent, and beautiful woman I've ever known. If anybody made you feel less than that, you tell me their name, and I'll break their nose. Nobody has the right to make you feel bad, Sunny. Never again."

She looked a bit surprised at his vehemence. Frankly, he was surprised at his own emotional outburst. His inner cat was running rampant over his better sense today. The little fur ball was getting him in deeper and deeper, and he only hoped it wouldn't scare off the love of his life.

"That's really sweet, Den, but I don't want you to break anybody's nose. Still, it's kind of nice of you to offer."

Relief coursed through him. She didn't think he was bonkers for reacting so strongly. Thank goodness.

"I just want you to know how special you are." He had to try again. To make his thoughts a little clearer and maybe not so insane. "I want to spend a lot more time with you, if that's what you want too. I want to see where this thing between us goes. I have a feeling it could lead to something really special. Something I've wanted for a long time."

Her breath caught in her throat, and she looked a little flushed. He'd pressed about as far as he could for now, so he backed off. Den turned his attention to his second sandwich and devoured it while she nibbled on the second half of her one and only sandwich. She was so thin he was half afraid she might blow away on the wind. Feeding her was going to become one of his favorite past times, he thought to himself with an inner chuckle. He liked providing for his mate. His inner fur ball began to purr at the very idea.

*

Den landed the plane on a small airstrip in the mountains. It didn't seem possible there was an airport this high up, but there it was. It came complete with a couple of hangars built into the side of the mountain and a small building where there were vending machines, toilets and an office manned by someone who answered to the name of Bubba.

Bubba greeted Den like an old friend, and Den introduced the man to Sunny, claiming they were old colleagues. Bubba told Den that he could take the truck and just send one of the youngsters back with it later, which seemed like a lot of trust to have in someone who wasn't yet part of their elite group, as Den had described it to Sunny.

"Everybody's up at the Pack house," Bubba told Den as he handed him the keys. "Best go up there first." He nodded toward Sunny, and Den nodded back.

Sunny suspected there was some unspoken message being passed regarding her presence, but she didn't really mind. She was very aware that she was on shifter territory here. She was a guest, and she didn't really understand their society. She only hoped she didn't make some egregious faux pas because she didn't know much about them or their traditions.

They got in the pickup truck, and Den drove off as if he knew exactly where they were headed. She guessed he had been here before and knew the lay of the land. That was handy.

Sunny was really starting to feel the exertion of the past hours. She reached into her bag and found the painkillers she detested but still needed, from time to time. When the pills rattled in their plastic bottle, Den looked over and frowned.

"I'm sorry, princess. Are you okay?" Now, he looked concerned.

"Yeah, I'll be all right. I just get really stiff when I don't move around enough, and sometimes, it hurts." She rattled the bottle of pills and made a face. "I hate these things, but sometimes, they really do help. I've weaned myself off of them, for the most part, but I still do need to take them occasionally."

Den looked grim when she peered over at him. "I'm really sorry. You move so well that I forget what you've been through. I promise to take better care of you from now on."

His words really surprised her. It was as if he felt somehow responsible for her physical condition. His concern was nice but unnecessary. She had been taking care of herself for a long time. Her parents had helped her through the worst of the injuries from her accident, but her recuperation was her responsibility. No one could do it for her. Physical therapists had helped, as had the medical people, especially the doctors who had put her back together again after the accident, but the rest was up to her. She had accepted that long ago.

She was still processing her thoughts when he rounded a

curve and turned onto a much smaller road. It was a driveway, she realized. Within moments, a very large house appeared before them, and he parked the car not far from the entrance. Then, he turned to her.

"Do you want to take one of those now," he asked, gesturing toward the pill bottle still in her hand, "or can it wait until we're inside?"

"Inside," she decided, putting the bottle back into her bag.

Maybe she wouldn't need it after she moved around a little. If she could just work out the kinks in her muscles, maybe the pain would go down to a tolerable level. Den nodded and got out of the truck. Before she could even open her door, he came around to the passenger side and opened it for her. He helped her down from the high truck with solicitous attention.

As her feet hit the ground, the front door of the home opened, and a familiar woman came down the steps. A woman Sunny had already met via a video call.

"Sally?" Sunny asked, surprised to find the former detective here in Wyoming. Sunny recalled she hadn't really asked where Sally was. She'd just assumed Sally was somewhere on the West Coast.

"Sunny." Sally paused a few feet from Sunny and just looked at her. "I'm so glad to see you in person. I didn't quite know how to talk to you about the serious stuff over video. The thing is…"

Sunny had a sudden flash of insight. Her mouth opened, and words came out that only registered as she spoke them.

"You're my family." There was no doubt in Sunny's mind.

CHAPTER 12

She had thought Sally looked awfully familiar when they had spoken earlier, but she couldn't place why or how. Now that they were face-to-face, it was obvious. They were related. Somehow, Sunny actually had living family. It was a minor miracle, and something she had never expected would happen.

"I'm your sister," Sally admitted, and the final piece of the puzzle settled into place. Yes. That felt right.

"I never knew I had a sister," Sunny admitted, tears gathering behind her eyes. They were happy tears, to be sure.

"I never did either," Sally replied. "It wasn't until I saw the family tree that I knew."

"Den did say something about a family tree, but I've never heard of such a thing. I don't really know much about what I am or what I can do. Besides making flowers bloom and talking to the trees, that is."

"That's already a lot. I grew up and lived for most of my life in the city. Until I came here, I didn't really know much about trees at all. I had never heard their song. But I always did have a way with plants and gardens. I had just never been in a forest or understood the complex nature of its organization."

Sunny was feeling stunned. "I can't believe I have family. I can't believe you're my sister," she whispered.

That did it. Sally rushed forward, and Sunny met her, and they hugged and hugged. Tears flowed, laughter burbled, and a smile stretched Sunny's face so wide she thought it might stay that way forever. When they finally broke apart, long minutes later, Sally kept her arm around Sunny's shoulders and turned her toward the house.

"Come on, I want you to meet everybody. Especially your brother-in-law." Sally laughed, and Sunny couldn't help but join in. They walked up the steps arm in arm, and Sunny was aware of Den following behind with her overnight bag.

Sally led the way into the big house, introducing Sunny to everyone they encountered. Sunny was fairly certain she was going to have trouble remembering all the names, but she tried her best. Sally led her back through the house along a long hallway that led to a closed door. She knocked once and opened it, and Sally could see it was an office.

A handsome man sat behind a large mahogany desk. He was on the phone, but the minute he saw Sally, he ended the call and stood. He walked around the desk, and Sally let go of Sunny, moving into his arms, hugging him tight. After a moment, she turned in the man's arms and faced Sunny.

"Sunny, this is Jason, my mate. Jason, this is my baby sister, Sunny." Pride sounded in every syllable, and Sally's expression was filled with joy.

Sunny felt not only welcomed but cherished, and tears threatened again. She had a feeling this was going to be a very emotional day.

Jason leaned forward, holding out his hand towards Sunny. She took it, liking the firm hand grasp and tempered strength of the man. It was clear he loved Sally a great deal.

"Pleased to meet you, Sunny. Welcome to the family." His smile was warm and open, and she felt tears gather again.

Yep. Today was going to be a teary one, but in the best possible way.

"It's great to meet you too, Jason. Alpha. I'm sorry. I don't know much about Pack life or etiquette, except for the little that Den has told me. Please forgive me if I make mistakes. I promise to learn, if you give me a chance."

"You're family," Jason said firmly. "You can't do anything wrong. Not here. And don't worry. Within a few days, you'll know more about Pack life than you probably want to know." Reassured by his attitude and good will, Sunny relaxed a little. "Now, how about I take Den off to chat with my brother and his guys while you two catch up?" Jason moved around Sally, leaving her with a peck on the cheek and motioned to Den.

"I'll just leave your bag here for now," Den told Sunny, putting her overnight bag on the table next to the couch along the side wall of the big office. "Do you need anything? Water? Something to eat?" he asked solicitously, and she remembered she had been going to take one of her pain pills.

But, she realized, she didn't need it now. The pain had receded, as she had hoped it would, with movement.

"No, it's okay," she told Den, smiling at him. He was such a good man. So thoughtful of her comfort. "I'll be fine. Thank you though."

Den tipped his imaginary hat to her. "All part of the service, ma'am."

She laughed at his reply, and he followed the Alpha wolf out the door, closing it behind him. That left her with her long-lost sister, Sally.

"Boy, have I got a lot to tell you," Sally said.

Sunny couldn't wait to learn what Sally knew about their mysterious shared origins.

*

Den went out of the office with Jason, shaking his head. He really did need to speak with both Jason and Jesse. Since meeting Sunny, his circumstances had changed drastically.

Finding one's mate changed everything. Jason and Jesse both had mates. They would understand. He also needed to brief them on what he had been able to discover about the attacks on Sunny. Brian had been doing some digging as well as surveillance, and he had forwarded his findings. It made for interesting reading. Den hadn't had a chance to look at it all yet, but the little bit he'd seen as he scrolled through email on his phone had piqued his interest.

To his surprise, Jesse and his mate, Maria, were waiting in the common room of the Pack house, sipping coffee. Jesse was a lot more relaxed since finding his mate, and Den had been jealous of the man until just recently. Now, Den fully understood that satisfied look on Jesse's face and the way his intense manner had changed.

A mate did that. She made life easier. She brought joy and peace where there had only been tension and work before. Den understood now, after finding Sunny, that there was so much more to life. She was his reason for living now. Even if she never accepted him as her mate, he would love no other. Sunny was it for him, and only her happiness mattered.

"I suspect you have something to tell us," Jason said as they arrived at the table where Jesse and Maria were sitting.

"I'll leave you boys to it," Maria offered, standing. "I want to check on a few things while I'm here."

Den knew that Maria was a doctor. A veterinarian, actually. She looked after animals and, since joining the Pack, people who could turn into animals. Caring for others was part of her nature and her calling. Den remained standing until Maria had left, then sat across from Jesse, next to Jason. He made sure he had their full attention before he dropped his bombshell.

"Sunny doesn't know it yet, but she is my mate." There. He'd said it out loud.

Den hadn't really planned that these men should be the first to find out, but he didn't really mind. The Moore brothers had been friends of Den's for years. They were close. So close that Den had been seriously seeking to join their Pack. A cougar among wolves. It seemed incongruous, but it would have worked.

Now that he'd found Sunny, though, he had to take her comfort into consideration in all things. Her adoptive parents lived in Sacramento. She might very well want to stay there to be near them. Or she might want to move to Wyoming to be with her sister. Until they'd had time to talk about things and make some decisions, everything was up in the air.

The Moore brothers congratulated Den. He could tell they were sincerely happy for him. Every shifter understood how important, special, and rare it was to find one's mate.

"I guess this means we're all family now," Jason said. "Our mates are both related to yours."

"Hot damn, we've got a cat in the family," Jesse said, grinning like a fool.

"Just remember this cat has claws and can climb trees," Den teased back, all in good fun.

They all laughed then got down to business.

"By the way, there never really was any question," Jesse stated, looking at Den. "Your spot in the Wraiths was pretty much guaranteed. If you still want it, it's yours. But I suspect your new mate will have something to say about your decision, and I completely understand that."

"Thanks, Jesse." Den felt honored to know that he had been so easily accepted among the elite group. "And you're right. It's going to depend on where Sunny wants to go and what she wants to do."

"Understood. I just wanted you to know you're welcome on the team, if you still want in." Jesse nodded, and Den nodded back. There was no need to say any more on the matter.

"Now, about this threat to your mate." Jason changed the subject.

What followed was a long discussion about everything they had been able to learn in the short time they'd had to study the problem. Much to Den's surprise and relief, both Jesse and Jason had set their people to work on the issue as soon as they'd found out about the danger Sunny was in. He was gratified to learn they'd put so much effort into Sunny's safety even before they'd met her. Then again, she was related to both of their mates, even though they'd never met. Sunny was important to their mates, which made her important to them as well. That's how it worked among shifters and one of the reasons why the Packs and Clans were all so tightly knit.

Den stayed with the men for a few hours, discussing matters.

They devised a plan that gave Den hope in case trouble had followed them all the way here. He didn't think it had, but just in case, it was good to know the Pack would have their backs. He also broached the subject of Sunny's parents. They were still away at their art retreat, but they were due to return to their ranch in just a couple of days.

Brian had reported that the intruders had made their way onto the ranch property but left when they realized Sunny had escaped. Still, the ward had been breached, and the ranch wasn't really safe anymore. Not until the ward was replaced with something stronger, if possible.

Jason was going to see how it worked out between Sally and Sunny, though indications right now were very positive. He had his feelers out, as did Jesse, to investigate the people who had adopted Sunny more in-depth. They'd already done a cursory investigation, just to find Sunny, but no one had turned up any information that Sunny's adoptive parents were magical.

From all appearances—and the existence of the ward around their property—it seemed that they were. They might be flying low under the radar, but there was magic there. Or at least the understanding of magic. Either way, more needed to be known about the people who had adopted Sunny. If they checked out, Jason had suggested they might be welcome to visit the Pack house, which was a big step.

It was rare for a wolf Pack to allow strangers into the heart of their territory, and the Pack house was most definitely the heart of this group. It was a place that allowed the group to gather together and share communal meals and celebrations. In large Packs, like this one, there was also always space for those who needed a place to stay. Jason had extended the invitation to Den and Sunny to stay there, in fact, which was both a statement of trust and friendship.

*

Sunny felt like she was living a dream. Sally was everything she ever could have wished for in a sister. Not that she'd ever known she actually had a sister. Her past had been a complete mystery until now. Actually, it still was a mystery, though she felt in her heart that Sally really was her sister. There was just a sort of instant recognition that told her it was true.

Sally had taken her outside to talk quietly on the wide back deck that led down from the Pack house into the nearby woods. They had both admitted to being more comfortable outside where they could hear the whisper of the wind through the trees.

"I could show you where Leonora is waiting," Sally offered. "It's not too far, as the crow flies. We could walk there."

Sunny wanted to go, but she was concerned about her limitations. Since her accident, she couldn't really move that well, or as fast as other people. Yet, she hated to admit her weakness to this vibrant woman. Sunny wanted her newfound sister to like her, not to pity her.

"Maybe a leisurely stroll?" Sunny asked hopefully. "I was cooped up in the cockpit for a bit too long, and I'm still feeling rather stiff."

"Sure thing. There's no rush. It's a nice walk. We just have to be back here by dinner, or the men will make a fuss." Sally made a face, and Sunny laughed as they both stood from their seats and headed down the steps of the wide deck that ran the length of the back of the Pack house.

"There's a wolf following us," Sunny said after they'd entered the trees. She wasn't worried, exactly, but she didn't know the rules of this place yet. The trees didn't seem all that concerned, so she wasn't worried, just unsure.

"Oh, that's just Arlo. He's one of Jesse's guys," Sally said off-handedly. "Apparently, even the Alpha bitch isn't quite free to roam alone on Pack lands." Sally raised her voice so the wolf following them could hear, then rolled her eyes. "These guys still don't get it. I was a cop. I still go around armed. I am fully able to take care of myself, but they insist I have a babysitter if I step a foot away from Jason." Sally stopped walking and shut her eyes, shaking her head as if in frustration, then reopened her eyes. "Okay. I know it's a sign of respect and care. I get it. It's just…hard to get used to. I was always a very independent woman. When you grow up in foster care, you learn to take care of yourself. Having a shadow all the time just feels a little stifling."

A giant wolf trotted out of the trees alongside their path and sat at Sally's feet, looking up at her with an adoring expression on his furry face. Sally looked down at him and wasn't able to keep from smiling.

"Arlo, you are an infuriating man. You know I can't ever stay mad at you when you do the hurt puppy routine. Though how something as enormous and deadly as you can carry it off, I'll never understand. Come along, if you wish." Sally turned to her and asked, "You don't mind, do you, Sunny?"

CHAPTER 13

"I don't mind," Sunny replied, eyeing the giant wolf with a healthy respect.

The trees said he was okay, so she wasn't afraid...exactly. But she was keeping a wary distance from the giant wild creature. She had never seen such an enormous wolf in her life! In fact, she'd never seen any wolf up close, but this one was gigantic.

They walked along for a while, the wolf bounding ahead at times then falling back to dog their steps. Literally. Sunny had never had a dog. Her parents had a small colony of barn cats on the ranch, but no dogs. They'd had a few other kinds of animals at various times. A few chickens, a trio of alpacas and a pet potbellied pig someone had asked them to take since it had outgrown their place.

Sally walked with Arlo, and Sunny was finding it hard to keep up, but she didn't want to say anything. She just did her best to ignore the pain and keep moving.

Suddenly, Sally stopped short. She turned to eye Sunny with suspicion.

"Why are the trees telling me to slow down for you?"

"Uh..." Sunny thought for sure Sally had known about her accident, but maybe she'd taken too much for granted. "Didn't Den tell you I'd been in a car wreck?"

"I read the report on the accident, but I didn't realize you had lasting damage. Den didn't go into that kind of detail. He wanted me to look into whether or not it really had been an accident. He seems to suspect it wasn't." Sally stilled, her gaze filled with apology. "I'm really sorry. I didn't realize you were still hurting. Do you want to go back? I mean—"

"How far is Leonora's willow from here?" Sunny cut off her newfound sister's awkward words with her question. Sunny hated being a cripple. She hated everyone's pity even more.

"From here?" Sally looked in the direction they'd been walking. "It's not far. Less than five minutes, even if we take it slower."

"Then, let's press on. I'd like to see the spot. We'll just take the walk back at an easier pace, and I'll be fine." She would be fine if she had to use every last shred of her will to make it that way. Sunny refused to give in to the pain, but she was going to be sensible about the rest of the walk, now that Sally understood a bit about Sunny's limitations.

She hated having any attention on her lack of mobility, but she had to deal with it like an adult. Sally had just been walking too fast over the rough terrain of the forest floor. While Sunny got some kind of energetic boost from being in the forest that she didn't fully understand, all the broken bones that had been repaired inside her just wouldn't let her move the way she used to. She would never dance again. Not as she had.

Sunny had spent a lot of time crying about that, but the doctors had all told her she should be thrilled that she was even walking at all without supports. Most of them had thought she would never walk again, and they had made no secret of their prognosis. She had proved them all wrong and was not only walking, but able to teach dance in some small capacity. Her legs might never be able to do a *grande jete* ever again, but she could teach the little ones the basics. And, with careful, slow movements, she could dance among the trees and make the flowers bloom.

When they finally arrived at the spot, Sunny could feel a change in the forest energies. They were in a grove that held a number of willow trees, but she knew without being told which one was the special one. The one that held the body of the dryad, Leonora, in suspended animation. Sunny walked right up to that very special willow and reached out hesitantly to put her hand on the bark of the trunk.

Its power welcomed her, and she felt a warmth go through her body, filling it with happiness. It was the happiness of the dryad trapped within the tree for her own safety. Leonora didn't speak in words, but Sunny understood her joy, nonetheless.

"She's not really here," Sunny said as she backed away from the tree, breaking the contact. "But she knows I'm here. It's like she's half here and half somewhere else, but her spirit is aware. You were telling the truth about all of it, incredible as it still seems to me."

Sally eyed her, nodding. "It's wise to be cautious. I'm glad you're checking out my story for yourself. If we'd grown up together, I would've taught you to be your own woman and not to trust anyone at first glance."

It occurred to Sunny that her older sister must have had a rough life as a youngster. Sunny had been fortunate enough to be adopted at a young age. Her parents had protected her from all the ugliness of life. They'd indulged her desire to dance and make sure she never wanted for anything. Especially love. She knew deep down in her heart that they loved her. As she loved them, in return.

Sunny was contemplating how to respond when someone joined them. Sally turned to greet another woman, and Sunny instantly saw the resemblance. This must be the cousin Den had mentioned.

"Maria, come meet my sister, Sunny," Sally invited,

gesturing to the other woman as she stepped closer. Maria moved to stand right in front of Sunny and held out her hand.

"Doctor Maria Garibaldi," she introduced herself. "I'm so glad to meet you."

Sunny took Maria's hand and felt a little tingle of magic at her touch. It was a soothing feeling, and Sunny remembered Den telling her that Maria was a veterinarian. Maria's brows furrowed as she stepped a tiny bit closer and looked more intensely at Sunny.

"You're in pain," Maria said, her voice a low murmur, almost as if she was talking to herself. "You have a lot of scar tissue in inconvenient places. Was it a car accident?"

"Yes," Sunny answered with some surprise.

"Hang on a second," Maria told her. "Just bear with me, and I think I can take away some of the pain."

Sunny didn't know what to expect, but Maria was just holding her hand, so Sunny didn't feel threatened in any way. Quite the contrary. Maria had a gentle manner about her that felt completely unthreatening.

Sunny felt the tingling between their hands grow to a bubbling sort of heat that didn't burn. It went up her arm, through her torso, and then coursed down her legs, bringing blessed relief. Sunny hadn't felt so good since before her accident. She had gotten used to the constant discomfort and just worked through it, but suddenly, a lot of it was just...gone. Gone as if it had never been. Sunny was stunned.

"What did you do?" Sunny asked as Maria finally let go of her hand and stepped back. The other woman was smiling, though she looked a bit weary.

"Our energies seem to like each other," Maria commented. "I meant to soothe some of the scar tissue, but I think, maybe, it did a bit more than that. Time will tell. But you do feel better, don't you?"

"So much better," Sunny admitted gleefully as she moved her limbs experimentally, stretching a bit more than she had since the accident had taken so much of her range of motion.

"Is this going to last? Is it permanent?" She tried really hard not to get her hopes up. This could just be a temporary reprieve. Either way, she would be thankful. It felt so good to be able to move a little better.

Maria was nodding. "Yes, it should be permanent. We can try again later, when my energies have rebuilt themselves a bit. I'm amazed you were even walking at all. There was a great deal of damage done to you, cousin." Maria frowned again, followed by a small smile. "I'm just glad I was able to help a little. Maybe we can do more tomorrow."

Sunny was about ready to cry from joy. This woman, this cousin of hers she'd never met before, had just given her the greatest gift. Sunny could move more freely than she had in almost a year. A tear ran down her face to drop into the loamy earth at the base of the willow tree. And where the tear had fallen, a flower sprang up and bloomed.

All three of the dryad's descendants smiled and laughed with each other. They all understood the power of their kind of magic. Joy always brought flowers where Sunny was concerned. This time, it was her favorite. A columbine, whose shape always brought to mind a shooting star.

"Thank you," Sunny said sincerely, reaching out to Maria to grasp her hands. "Thank you so much. You have no idea what this means to me. I will never forget your generosity."

"I didn't get a chance to tell you," Sally said to Maria, moving to stand next to her. "My little sister was a professional dancer before her accident. She was a prima ballerina."

Sunny let go of Maria's hands and nodded. "The accident ended my career. I haven't been able to dance—not really dance—since. I've been deep in grief over the loss of the greatest joy I had in life. I loved dancing. And my magic was often expressed through movement. I used to go out and dance among the trees on our ranch, but I haven't really been able to do that. Not like I used to. The pain has been too intense at times."

"And yet, you were walking, even with the pain," Maria

reminded her. "I take it you walked from the Pack house to here?"

Sunny nodded in reply. "I had to ask Sally to slow down a little bit," she admitted with some embarrassment.

"But you still walked all that distance," Maria stated. "You must have a will of iron, Sunny. Since I've discovered the true nature of my gifts, I've been able to expand my abilities beyond what they once were. I could tell just by touching your hand how much pain you were in and how much damage had been done to your body. To your bones. I have to say, most people would not have achieved as much as you have with all that damage. You should be proud of yourself. But, now that I know about it, and I know you, we can work together to fix more of that damage. You don't have to be in so much pain all the time. Human medicine did what it could for you, but now, it's time to try a little magic."

"Den said something like that," Sunny said, wonder in her voice. "And his sister promised she would try to find help for me, if I didn't find it here."

"You've met Den's family already?" Sally asked, her eyebrows raised.

"His sister is married to the foreman of the work crew that's revitalizing part of Sacramento. When Den and I fled from my family's ranch, he took me to the beautiful old Victorian they had restored and were living in while they worked on the rest of the houses they had bought in the area. Den's sister was really nice, and her husband is a bear shifter," Sunny told her newfound family.

She realized the wolf, Arlo, had held back and allowed them some space. She suspected he could still hear what they said, though. Wolf hearing had to be pretty keen.

"Is it serious, between you two?" Maria wanted to know.

Sunny blushed and looked down at her feet. "I guess. I mean, I don't know exactly, but…"

When Sunny looked up again, both women were smiling at her.

"In my experience, when shifter men get all cagey about

the status of a relationship, it usually means they're getting very serious, indeed," Sally teased. "If it wasn't serious, you would know that. These shifters don't play games with people's hearts. But, if they are serious, they tend to get very, very cautious, to the point of not saying anything and driving you crazy wondering whether they really care or not." Some of the frustration Sally must've felt in her own mating came through in her words, but it wasn't angry or anything like that. If anything, Sally sounded amused by her husband's antics in courting her.

"I guess this means we're going to have a cat in the family." Maria was beaming, her eyes alight with amusement.

"I don't know about that," Sunny objected, looking down again with a bit of embarrassment.

Surely, they were getting carried away. She had only known Den for a couple of days, and they'd been some of the most tumultuous days of her life, aside from the accident and the immediate aftermath.

"Mark my words, I think our wolves are just going to have to get used to having your cat around," Sally said with a wide grin.

"Oh, but they're old friends. Den was going to join the Wraiths anyway. He's been discussing it with Jesse and Jason for a while," Sunny revealed, much to the other women's surprise.

"You don't say?" Maria asked, speculation gleaming in her eyes. "This gets better and better."

"I hope you know you're welcome here, Sunny," Sally stepped in, her expression earnest. "You're my sister."

A little thrill went through Sunny to hear that word. She still couldn't quite believe it.

"And my cousin," Maria added. "We both live here. Well, I live up the mountain a ways in the Wraith encampment, since my mate leads them, but we live in the same Pack territory and see each other all the time."

"You are welcome to live here, as well, though I know you have your adoptive parents to consider," Sally went on, picking up the thread. "I want you to know how thankful I am that you had a good childhood and a good life with your parents. I'm glad you knew that kind of love and caring. I just… I want to be part of your life and have you be part of mine now that we know about each other. I won't push, but think about it, okay?"

Sunny didn't really have to think about that. She definitely wanted her sister and cousin in her life now that she'd met them, but she did have her parents to consider. Their home was in Sacramento—though their home had been invaded by evil. Maybe her folks wouldn't want to stay there after that. She'd have to have a serious talk with them about it and their options.

"I want you both in my life. That's a no-brainer," Sunny told them. "As for the rest, I have a lot to think about. And I really need to talk to my folks. Things happened at home. Bad things. I'm not sure what that will mean long-term."

"You know," Sally began slowly, as if thinking through her words as she spoke them, "I've been thinking about this. Your folks are supposed to return to Sacramento tomorrow, right? What if we redirected them here? I mean, I haven't run this past Jason yet, but if he objects to bringing them onto Pack lands, then we can put them up nearby. Thing is, we can bring them to Wyoming and look after them. Maybe facilitate that serious discussion you all need to have and help figure out how to safeguard them if they do decide to go back to the ranch and stay. Jason and Den, for that matter, have a lot of connections."

"Den's got that whole construction crew already in place in Sacramento," Sunny said, thinking aloud. "I think they would help, at least for a short time. I don't think they're staying any longer than it takes to get the houses finished, and that should happen in the next few months, I believe." Sunny bit her lip then released it. "I've been worrying about my folks returning to the ranch now that the bad guys know about it. I've been feeling more and more like it's not the safe haven it once was."

"I hate to say this, but you're probably right," Maria said, sighing. "I had to give up my sanctuary when the enemy found out where I lived. Of course, I mated with Jesse soon after, so it was just natural that I move here to be with him. I had to find homes for almost all of my animals though. I ran a rehab for exotic and wild animals. Not all of them could make the trip here, and not all would be comfortable around so many wolves, but eventually, it all worked out."

"The thing is," Sally spoke into the silence that followed Maria's words, "we're going to need you here when we attempt to get Leonora out of the willow and heal her. I mean... You don't have to stay the whole time, if you don't want to, but when we finally have the group together, we're going to need for all of us to be here together to do the magic."

"What exactly are we going to do? And how many others do we need? And how did Leonora get stuck in the willow in the first place?" Sunny had so many questions!

CHAPTER 14

"I put her in the willow to preserve her life. She'd been shot with a silver bullet, and the poison of it was killing her fast. The local Master vampire, Dmitri was here, and he gave her a few drops of his blood to prolong her life, and then, I put her into the willow so it would protect and preserve her until we were ready," Sally explained. "I've been researching it ever since and talking it over with the High Priestess, Bettina. We believe what we need to do is something called the Elven Star. It will require seven of us. Seven of the dryad's descendants. With you, Sunny, we now have four. Myself, Maria, you, and our cousin Cecelia. She lives in Northern California, but she's promised to come when we need her. She just married too, so she's more or less on her honeymoon."

"So, we need three more? And, forgive me, did you just say there was a vampire involved? They're real?" Sunny was shocked.

"As real as you and me," Sally replied immediately. "The local Master is actually a great guy. He married one of my dearest friends a while back, and that's what brought me out here to Wyoming to check on her and meet the guy. I didn't know he was a vampire when I first got here, but the secret came out relatively fast, and Dmitri and Carly enlisted Jason to show me around during the day when they were asleep."

"Your friend is a vampire too?" Sunny asked, intrigued.

"She is now, but she wasn't when I knew her. We became friends in college. There was a whole group of us, and all the others ended up with vampires, which is statistically odd, but I got myself a werewolf, so I broke the pattern," Sally explained with a grin. "All in all, I'm happy for Carly and Dmitri. They're very much in love, and they both deserve happiness. You'll get to meet them one of these nights if you stick around here long enough. They only bite each other now that they've mated, so no worries on the getting bitten thing. Although, Dmitri did mention that dryad blood was like nectar to his kind. When she got shot, Leonora's blood was a sort of clear pale green, like tree sap or something. I bleed red, like regular people. I assume you do too, right?" The others nodded agreement. "Our dryad heritage is very dilute, which is why I think it'll take so many of us to do the magic we need to do to save Leonora."

They spent a few more minutes talking, but the amount of information Sunny was being given, all at once, was close to blowing her mind. Her parents had never really talked too much about the magical world, preferring to let her learn on her own, if she could. Oh, she knew they believed in many fantastical things, but they had really never discussed anything in great detail with her. They had usually shied away from talking about magic in anything other than the fairytale sense as she grew up.

Now that she had time to think about it, that seemed odd to her. Especially considering the ward—whatever that really was—that Den had claimed had been set around the ranch. She'd seen it for herself when that red energy bounced off of a sort of invisible dome that had covered the ranch property. Sunny couldn't deny the evidence of her own eyes. Her parents had some explaining to do the next time she saw them.

The four of them walked back to the Pack house together. Arlo, in wolf form, loped along in front or behind them, acting as a guard, while Sunny, Sally and Maria strolled along, enjoying the forest and chatting.

By the time they arrived, it was nearly dinnertime. Sunny hadn't realized how much time they'd spent out in the woods. She often lost track of time when she was out in nature, particularly among trees. That all started to make sense now that she knew about her heritage.

Den was about ready to send out a search party when Sunny finally arrived back at the Pack house with Sally and Maria. He had been in a strategy session all afternoon, but they had decided on a plan and ended the meeting not too long ago. He'd immediately gone looking for Sunny, only to be told she was still out walking in the woods with her sister.

He knew, intellectually, that she wouldn't come to any harm on Pack lands, but he still wanted to see her. To be sure that she was safe. It was a need in his soul to be certain that she was all right. He had just barely been able to restrain himself from going after her because he knew that Arlo was acting as their bodyguard. He knew and trusted Arlo, but that didn't make him any happier not having Sunny where he could see her.

When she came in the back door, he rose from his seat and went over to her. He couldn't help himself. He drew her into his arms for a quick hug. He tried to make it nonchalant, but he was afraid she might have noticed the trembling in his arms. His relief was palpable.

Den had heard about this sort of thing. The newly mated often found it difficult to be separated for any length of time. Especially in the beginning. And perhaps, especially since Sunny didn't even know that they were mates yet, Den felt really insecure about that. She wasn't a shifter. What if she didn't feel the same about him? It would kill him. Literally.

He needed her in his life. He needed her so badly that he would do anything to make sure that she was happy. He would even keep his distance, if that's what she really wanted.

He wouldn't like it, and it might just drive him mad, but he would watch over her from afar if she truly believed there was no way they could be together. Until their relationship was settled, one way or another, he was going to be a little more intense than usual. He supposed the other guys knew this—especially the mated ones—and they were either laughing behind their backs at him or full of compassion for his plight. Probably a little bit of both.

"Did you have a nice walk in the forest?" Den made himself let go of her and stepped back a pace.

"Did you know there was a vampire living nearby? I didn't even know they really existed! There's so much I have to learn." Sunny shook her head, a look of disbelief on her face.

Den relaxed. She hadn't noticed his worry. She seemed preoccupied with everything Sally had to have told her.

"There are stranger things in heaven and earth," he paraphrased the Bard. "You know you can ask me anything, right? I know a lot of this is new to you. I'll be happy to answer anything I can."

"Thanks." She met his gaze, her eyes still full of wonder at everything she had talked about with her sister. "Did you know that Maria is my cousin?"

"I did. I'm glad you got a chance to meet her. She's a very nice woman and, by all accounts, a fine veterinarian." Den didn't know much more about Maria, though he had met her a few times. She was a little quieter personality than Sally and probably took a bit longer to get to know.

"She's some kind of healer, actually." Sunny reached out and grasped his forearm. "Den, she did something to me. She took away a lot of the pain I've been feeling for so long. When we walked back, it was like I was a new person, and she says it's permanent. She thinks she can do even more once she's had a chance to recharge her batteries. Den," she almost gasped with excitement, "I might be able to dance

117

again. Not professionally, of course. Those days are over. But I never really cared for the spotlight anyway. I danced for the sake of dance, and I have missed it. Oh, how I have missed it."

Den was amazed. He hadn't known that Maria was a healer in addition to being a veterinarian. It made sense that she would go into that sort of field, if she had a healing talent. He didn't know much about these dryads. They all seemed to have different specialties. He assumed it was because they weren't full-blooded dryads. The other influences in their ancestry probably affected how their magic worked.

He was going to have to do something very special for Maria. She had worked a miracle and might even do more. Regardless, what she had done was give the spark of hope back to his mate. Sunny looked radiant and so full of wonder. He wanted to lean down and kiss her right there in front of everybody. He wanted to lift her into his arms and twirl her around in joy, but he restrained himself. There would be time for that later.

What he needed to do now was fill her in on the plans they had made earlier in the day. Some of it would affect her directly and needed her participation and approval.

"Sunny, I know you speak to your parents every night, and they're due to go back to their home in Sacramento soon, but Jason, Jesse, and I have been discussing things, and we think it might be better to have them come here instead of going home right away. It's pretty obvious they are aware of the magical world, even if they kept you somewhat in the dark about it. That ward around your home was very powerful, if I'm any judge of those sorts of things. I think we need to talk to them directly about all of this, and the threat. I can't be one hundred percent certain that the attack was meant solely for you. They might also be in danger." He wasn't happy about the shadows that entered her eyes at his words, but it was necessary. He had to be completely honest with his mate. "I can't imagine, after knowing you, that they would be involved in anything evil. I don't believe they could've raised you the way they did and been bad themselves. Jason is in agreement, though Jesse, as is his nature, is still skeptical. Regardless, it's better to have them here where we can talk to them and discover what's going on, than sending them back into possible danger. What do you think?"

"Sally said something similar," Sunny admitted in a small voice. "I've been thinking about it, and I think I'd better talk to them tonight and ask them to come here. Sally says Jason probably has contacts that can pick them up in a private plane and bring them here, without having to go home first. That would be a lot safer, considering what was going on when we left the ranch." Her voice grew stronger as she went along, and Den was pleased to see her bouncing back.

"Brian has been reporting in, and there was some activity at the ranch. They've left watchers there, probably hoping you would return. Or your parents. If these guys are who I think they are, then your parents wouldn't be safe with them either."

Den had taken Sunny to one side in the main room of the Pack house while the others had gone ahead to clean up before dinner. Others bustled in and out from the kitchen, setting tables and putting out condiments, but they were able to speak quietly without being overheard too much. Not that it would matter. Everyone would know soon enough that Sunny's folks had been invited here by the Alpha couple, for their own safety.

"It's hard to imagine. The ranch has been my safe place for so long. It really bothers me to think that people are trespassing there. But who do you think they are?" She turned her inquisitive gaze on him.

"I know this is all new to you, and you've already been bombarded with a lot of information, but there are a few more things you need to know. Chief among them is the existence of an ancient order of evil known as the *Venificus*."

He took her hand and led her to an empty table. They both sat, and he went on with his explanation.

"Centuries ago, there was a fey sorceress named Elspeth.

She wanted to take over the world. She came very close, in fact, to doing just that. But the forces of Light worked together to defeat her and her followers. It took many years, but the final result was that Elspeth was banished to the farthest realm, and her followers were either killed or disbanded. At least, everyone thought the *Venifucus* had disbanded." Den frowned as he related the tale. "In recent years, it's become clear that they did not. They've been working in secret to bring their leader back from the farthest realm and cause chaos here in the mortal realm. They've been behind a series of attacks on magic users, shifters, vampires, and all sorts of Others."

"But why? What would they gain from attacking me or my parents? Up until recently, I knew nothing about this magical world. I'm nobody. What can they hope to get from me?"

"Your power." He hated saying this. He hated having to expose her to the ugliness of the world around them, but she needed to know. "You have untrained magic within you, Sunny. As a descendent of a dryad, you have untapped elemental power, and that's not something easy to come by. There aren't many elemental powers in the world to begin with. Which makes you a very attractive target for someone evil and unscrupulous, who would drain you of every bit of your energy in horrific ways. By the end, you would be begging for death."

He let the silence stretch for a moment, hoping his warning was sinking in, despite the fact that he wished he never had to tell her about these things. Sunny was everything good and bright in the world. Telling her of the darkness, the ugliness, didn't appeal to him. He knew he had to do it, but he didn't like it. Knowledge was power and she needed to know to keep her safe. And her safety was of paramount importance to him.

"Do you think…?" She cleared her throat and tried again. "Do you think these people could be after my parents for the same reason? I mean, I don't know if they're magical, but you said there was a ward around the property." She looked so worried and lost, Den reached out to take her hands in his, offering comfort.

"That ward is what convinces me that they at least know *something* about magic, if they are not, indeed, magical themselves. Either way, we can't let them walk into a trap. It's clear that the *Venifucus*—if that's really who are staking out your ranch right now—are waiting for someone to show up. If they can't get you, they might take your folks instead." He hated the fear in her eyes.

"They're in danger because of me?"

CHAPTER 15

Sunny looked so lost, so afraid, Den wanted to take her into his arms and just rock her until she quieted, but that wouldn't solve anything. It would make him feel better for a while. Her too. But ultimately, they had to do something to fix this.

"Possibly." Den had to be scrupulously honest with her. That was the only way to be with your mate. "But it's also likely that they have magic of their own that they just never told you about, because you don't have the same kind of magic. Remember, that elemental power within you is something incredibly rare. I'd be surprised if they could recognize it for what it really is. The only reason we know about you, and exactly what you are, is because of Leonora and the family tree that she taught Sally how to produce. If not for that, I'm not sure anybody would've recognized you as a part-dryad. It's just not something people think of because it's so uncommon."

"All right." Sunny looked at the clock on the wall then back to him. "It's almost time for me to call my folks. I'd like you to be on the call, in case they need anything explained. It's about time they met you anyway. I don't like lying to them, even by omission."

"That's understandable. Even admirable. I'll help in whatever way I can, and yes, I'd like to meet them too, even if it's only via video chat."

She stood, and he followed suit. "If all goes as planned, you'll get to meet them in person soon enough."

Together, they headed out of the common room, toward the big main hallway. Sally was standing there, in the hallway, talking with Maria and Jesse. Sunny went right up to the group without hesitation. They were her family, after all, and she didn't know anything about shifter etiquette and Alphas. Not too many Others would be so willing to interrupt such a high-powered group.

Den held back while Sunny talked with her family. He could hear what they were saying, of course. He was a shifter, after all. Everybody knew any conversation held out in public, like this, was going to be overheard. It's just the way it was when everyone in the house was a shifter.

Except for those three women. Part-dryads, they had different gifts. And, from what Den had seen, their gifts were different from each other's, as well. He would spend the rest of his life enjoying his time with Sunny, if she agreed, learning all the quirks of her personality and power.

It was decided that Sunny would talk to her parents and invite them here. Sally revealed that Jason was already in his office, making phone calls to try and set up a private jet to get her parents and bring them here. All Sunny needed to do was break the news to her folks and get them to agree.

Sally escorted Sunny and Den to one of the guest suites on the second floor of the Pack house. Their stuff had already been delivered, and Sally left them there after reminding them both that dinner would be served in about an hour and a half. Sunny cranked up her laptop and signed into the Wi-Fi, connecting with her parents on the first try. Apparently, they'd been waiting for her call.

"Where are you?" her mother asked. "I don't recognize the room you're in."

Den had stayed out of the frame. Sunny was going to introduce him once she brought the conversation around to the critical stuff.

"I'm safe, that's the most important thing," Sunny started.

"What do you mean, you're safe? Why aren't you home at the ranch?" her father demanded.

Sunny turned the tables on them. "What do you really know about magic?"

Her parents both got very silent and just looked at her, blinking.

"What do you mean?" said her mother while her father asked, at the same time, "What happened?"

"I found out about the ward around the property. Some lunatic came calling with a bunch of friends and was lobbing dark red fireballs at it. It held long enough for me to escape, but I have to warn you, the ward is down." She let that sit for a moment, and Den had to admire the way she was handling this.

"How do you know about wards?" her father wanted to know.

Sunny sighed. "Well, I didn't know anything about them before last night. When somebody attacked our home, trying to get to me. Apparently, I'm part-dryad. I'm guessing from the surprised looks on your faces that you never realized that."

"We didn't," her mother admitted. "We sensed you were magical, but we never knew exactly how. If you had demonstrated any of the signs we were familiar with, we would've taken you into our school and taught you how to handle your magic. As it was, the only thing we ever saw was your ability to make flowers bloom. Neither of us are familiar with that, and frankly, it's not something taught in any mage school, so we hoped things would come clearer as you grew up."

Sunny was stunned. Her mother had just admitted to knowing all about magic. Something they had never discussed in a serious way. Not once.

"Well, it's clear now. I am the long-lost descendent of a dryad, and I have a little bit of that kind of power."

"How do you know this? Who have you been talking to?" her father asked, clearly concerned.

"It turns out, I have a sister. She sent someone to seek me out. His name is Den, and he's the one who helped me escape. He took me to my sister. Her name is Sally, and she's mated to a werewolf Alpha. I'm in their Pack territory, under their protection, and I didn't know about any of this stuff!"

Sunny's frustration boiled over for a quick minute, but she throttled it back. Her parents had done the best they could for her. They had kept her safe all these years. They hadn't understood her magic. She could understand that. Most of all, she knew they loved her and had tried their best to make a good life for her.

"You have a sister?" Her mother seemed near tears. "We didn't know. We tried to find out if there were any blood relations, but we were never able to find anyone. I hope you know, we would never keep you from your blood family, even though we love you as our daughter."

"And I love you too," Sunny was quick to reassure them. "Sally didn't know about me until recently. She was raised in foster care. She had a rough time of it. But she's really great. Before she married Jason, she was a police detective. She's actually pretty cool."

"I'm so glad for you, honey," her mother said with tears in her eyes. "But are you sure about this?"

Sunny nodded. "I knew her the moment I saw her in person. There's no mistaking that we are sisters. And I have a cousin here too. She's a veterinarian with a real healing gift. I can already walk better than I have since the accident, and she said she would do more tomorrow, maybe, once she regained her energy. She's fantastic and so nice."

Her dad still looked skeptical. "Are you sure they're all on the level? I'm always leery of people bearing gifts. What do they want from you, in return?"

"I've thought about that, Dad. And you're right. There is something they want from me, but it's my decision. When they've gathered enough of us, they want me to participate in a spell that will heal the dryad who is our ancestor. She was shot with a silver bullet and lays between realms in a sort of suspended animation until we can get enough of us together."

Now that she knew her parents understood magic, she wouldn't hold anything back from them. They might even be able to help.

"Sounds tricky. What school of magic do they belong to? Are they getting advice from anyone?" Her father looked as if he was puzzling out the problem. She was very familiar with that expression on his face. Her dad was more of a scholar than a doer.

"Nobody's mentioned anything about schools of magic. I know Sally said she's been talking to the High Priestess. That's where she got the idea for the Elven Star."

Sunny saw no reason to keep any of this a secret from her parents. Maybe she should've asked Sally, but Sunny felt in her heart that her parents were trustworthy, even if they hadn't told her about the magical world. She knew them. They had probably just been trying to protect her.

"The Elven Star?" Her father repeated the words as if he understood them. She suspected he probably did. "That's a very potent arrangement. But if you're working with the High Priestess, it makes sense. Only someone of that stature could control such a powerful situation."

"Do you know the High Priestess?" Sunny had to ask.

"We know of her," her mother admitted. "She is said to be one of the ancient powers. There are those who claim she is an immortal."

"Well, Sally seems to think she's really nice and willing to give us advice on how to help our ancestor." Sunny figured it was about time to call in Den and introduce him to her parents. She waved over at him. "Mom, Dad, I want you to meet Den."

He moved into the frame, sitting beside her on the edge of the bed. Sunny had dragged the side table over and set up her laptop on it for exactly this reason. This way, they could both talk to her folks at the same time.

Den exchanged greetings with her stunned parents. He was both polite and patient with them, which touched her heart. She knew them so well. She knew that they were having a hard time dealing with all the changes coming so quickly. Den gave them space and seemed to understand their surprise.

"The thing is," Den explained to them, "judging by what I saw of the enemy's abilities, it's probably not safe for you to return to your property just yet. We have an operative watching the place, and he's reported some enemy activity on your land since the fall of the ward."

Sunny's father looked grim. "That's not good. What kind of operative do you have watching the place? Who are your people?"

"Sir, I'll answer that because I'm involved with your daughter, but you have to understand these are not questions most shifters will answer." Den sounded patient, but it was clear he was indulging them because of her. "My birth Clan is Redstone. As you probably know, Redstone Construction has had a crew working in your area for the past few months. I'm not part of that crew, but my sister is mated to the foreman, and my mentor has been overseeing security for them. He's the one watching your property, and I know no one better skilled at surveillance than him. He's literally had centuries of experience."

"Then, you're a shifter?" her mother asked.

"Yes, ma'am. I'm actually a cougar, though that's another question most shifters will not answer. I'm guessing you two never had much experience with my kind?" Den phrased his question in a friendly manner and gave them a small smile to put them at ease.

Sunny's mother was shaking her head. "I've heard about

shifters, of course, but we don't mix with Others much. Hardly at all, in fact. We're not exactly…at the head of our hierarchy. Our kind of magic isn't really valued by our respective families. We founded our own school for those like us whose magic is expressed through art or other creative pursuits. It's not popular—or even recognized by the great families—and we hardly have any students, but we keep it going as a safe haven for those like us, who aren't really good with the combative arts. Our magic is protective. We're good at talismans, wards, and crafting magical items that help protect or shield their owners or users. The wards on our property are linked to small sculptures and other items you'll find around the perimeter, as an example. We've gotten better at it over the years, but our families didn't support our training or our desires to do magic through art, so we were slow starters. We have the hang of things now though, and we help others like ourselves, who fly under the radar of the great magical families and their ridiculous expectations."

Sunny suddenly understood so much more about her parents. They were kindhearted souls who couldn't hurt a fly. It was no wonder they had retreated to their ranch and made it a safe place for others like them. They were really good people.

Den seemed to understand as well. "The Alpha is extending an invitation to you both, to come here, rather than return to Sacramento right away. You would be granted safe passage through Pack lands and given a place to stay, free of charge. Sunny is already bound to this Pack because of her relation to the Alpha female of the overall Pack and the Alpha female of the sub-group that exists within the larger Pack." Den made a face and shook his head. "The structure of this group is a little complicated, but they're all good people, sworn to the Light. As long as you're on the right side of the old struggle between good and evil, you'll be safe here."

"We are, of course," her father answered. "I don't like letting evil run amok at our home, but I don't see a way we could oust them by ourselves. We don't have any offensive magic." He was frowning as he thought things through. "Marilisa and I need to talk this over, but I'm leaning toward taking the Alpha up on his offer. For one thing, I want to make sure Sunny is okay. I need to see you in person, sweetheart," he said, directly to Sunny. "If we had known this was going to happen, we never would've left you on your own. I hope you believe that."

"Of course, Dad. I know that."

Sunny suspected he was feeling guilty about having left her at home on her own, despite the fact that she had urged them to go. They hadn't left her side since the accident. They deserved a little time away. Or so she'd thought.

"We're about to have dinner," Den told them. "I think it's going to be a bit of a celebration to welcome Sunny to the Pack, so it should go on for a few hours. How about we call back after? Say, about eleven? I know the Alpha was working the phones when we came up here to make this call. By that time, he should have plans in place, and perhaps you'll have made your decision."

Sunny's parents were nodding. "That sounds fair. Thank you, Den. I'd like to meet you in person as well," her father said, his tone not entirely friendly.

He both sounded and looked suspicious when he glanced back and forth between Sunny and Den. Sunny tried not to squirm. Her father had given almost every one of her boyfriends a hard time when she was growing up and starting to date.

"I look forward to it, sir," Den replied, perfectly polite. "We'll call you back at eleven then." Den got up and left Sunny to say goodbye to her parents.

Her mother had a few more questions about her safety and if she was sure about all this, but Sunny reassured her as best she could. She hoped they would come to Wyoming. It would be so much easier to explain all of this in person, where they could meet the people involved and judge for themselves. She said as much to them, and they seemed to take it well. They said goodbye with the promise to talk later, and then, the connection closed.

Sunny sighed heavily and sat back. She closed the laptop but left it where it was. They would need it again in a few hours.

"That went well," Den said, standing by the foot of the bed, watching her.

"Yeah," she agreed. "I think it went as well as it could. I also think they're probably going to take Jason up on his offer to come out here."

CHAPTER 16

"I can't believe they knew about magic all this time and never discussed it with me." Sunny looked disgruntled, and Den came back to sit beside her and put his arm around her shoulders. "They didn't lie to me, per se, but it still feels a little bit like a betrayal. I mean, they knew since I was a little kid that I could make flowers grow and bloom, but all they did was tell me not to tell the other kids in school about it. They made me hide my ability, which makes total sense, considering it's not normal for a six-year-old to be making flowers bloom out of season, but they could've said something, you know?"

"It's obvious to me that they love you and thought they were doing what was best for you. I'll be interested to learn the extent and nature of their magic. I know a little bit about the way human mage schools are set up, but I will put out some feelers and get more information. It sounds to me like their families lean more toward combat mages, which is a bit worrying, to be honest." Den thought hard about what her parents had said. "It sounds like their magic comes through their art, somehow, though I've never heard of that before."

"They do a lot of commission work," Sunny told him. "They're not really famous or anything, but they have a very select clientele that pays pretty well for the work they produce. And from time to time, they'll have guests staying at the ranch, some of them long-term. Students, they called them, but usually, their art was in different forms. There was one guy who sculpted out of stone. He made the most beautiful things but, like, super quick. He'd go into the barn—they'd set one of the smaller outbuildings aside just for him—with a big boulder, and the next day, he'd show off some new creation that was incredibly detailed. I always wondered how he managed to do all that work in just one day. Even if he worked through the night, it didn't seem possible, but I was warned not to ask questions, and I was little, so I did as I was told." Sunny shook her head. "They weren't mean about it, and after a month or two, I never saw him again."

"What happened to his sculptures?" Den wondered if the magic went into their creation or were part of the artistic works, themselves. Was the power in the creating of it or in the object?

"Someone always came for them. Different people. I did see one in front of someone's house years later. It stood at the base of their front steps." Sunny sounded speculative. "It was facing outward almost like it was protecting the house or something."

"I wonder. Maybe it was." Den rubbed her upper arm in a soothing motion. "Do you remember any other students?"

"Yeah, there was this one lady. Her name was Miriam. She made jewelry. Gorgeous handcrafted stuff, using gold wire and precious stones. It was absolutely stunning and so glittery. I was fascinated by it when I was little. She gave me a necklace before she left, and I wore it only for special occasions. From what I understand, her pieces go for thousands. She's not exactly a household name, but she's apparently well known in certain circles. At least, that's what my mother always said." Sunny shook her head once more and sighed. "We'd better go down to dinner before Sally sends a search party after us."

"Just prepare yourself," Den warned with a wry chuckle. "It's not just dinner. It's a party. And if there's one thing shifters know how to do, it's throw a party. And you are the guest of honor. I suspect this is your Welcome to the Pack party."

"It is?" Sunny looked both apprehensive and joyful. She jumped up from the side of the bed and raced to her bag. "I've got to change! What am I going to wear?"

Den watched her rummage through her bag, thoroughly amused. She was gorgeous no matter what she wore, but this little bit of feminine vanity made him want to hug her tight and never let go. His inner cat was urging him on. He was going to have to talk to her about this soon. She had to realize how special she was to him, and his inner fur ball wanted some kind of commitment. So did his human side. He didn't want to go much longer without her knowing how important she was to him.

But tonight, the party was in her honor. He wanted her to enjoy it and enjoy this time with her newfound family. They would have another party—probably more than one—to celebrate their mating, if she accepted him.

Sunny got ready in a remarkably short period of time. She had a slinky black tunic dress in some kind of stretchy knit fabric that made her look like a million bucks. Dressed up with a brightly patterned scarf and a beautiful pendant around her neck, she was ready to party.

Den was proud to walk down the staircase with her on his arm. She really was moving a lot better than she had been, but she still needed a little extra care on the steps. Whatever Maria had done had worked wonders. The little lines of pain that had shown around her mouth since they'd first met were now gone, as if they had never been. He hoped and prayed that Maria could work some more of her healing magic and bring about a full recovery for Sunny.

He knew she wanted to dance again, and he wanted that for her. Movement and dance had been such a big part of her life, and he wanted that back so she could feel fulfilled. Even if she wanted to dance professionally again, he wouldn't deter her from it. Whatever she wanted, whatever made her feel fulfilled and whole, that's what he wanted for her. That's what being a mate—a true mate—was all about.

They entered the common room of the Pack house, and there were cheers and people waiting to welcome Sunny to the Pack. Jason made a little speech of official acceptance into the Pack and his family, and then, the women grabbed Sunny to introduce her around.

A buffet dinner had been set up, but this was the mixer part of the evening. They'd eat in a bit, then there might be music and dancing after. The party would go on for hours, and Den prepared to settle in for a night of watching his mate enjoy herself and her new family.

Den grabbed a beer and stood back, observing the proceedings. Tonight was Sunny's night to shine. To meet her extended Pack family and be made a fuss over by them all. He would watch over her. If she needed him, he'd be here for her, but otherwise, he was hanging back, enjoying her enjoyment.

"She's a very nice woman, your Sunny," Arlo commented, sidling up next to Den, a beer in his hand as well. "You did good bringing her here. She doesn't know much about what she is or how the real world works, but her sister and cousin did a good job telling her a few things earlier today."

"Thanks for guarding them while they were out in the woods," Den said. He knew Arlo from his days in the service and had always respected both the man and his skills.

"My pleasure," Arlo acknowledged. "I've got a soft spot for Sally and Maria. They've been really great additions to our Pack. They make us stronger, and they ground Jason and Jesse. It's good to have stability at the top of the hierarchy."

"I know what you mean. The Redstone brothers were always solid guys, but the Clan has only gotten stronger with the addition of their mates. Those ladies really add something to the Clan," Den agreed.

"You still giving thought to leaving Redstone and joining the Wraiths?" Arlo asked.

Den wasn't sure how to answer. "I was. I still am, I guess. The thing is…"

"Sunny," Arlo said with finality. "I thought so. Congratulations, my friend. Does she know yet?" Arlo was grinning as he looked from where Sunny stood with the other women to Den and back again.

"Not yet," Den admitted, knowing some of his nerves about that were showing. "Jason and Jesse know, but nobody else. Except you now. I wanted to give her time to get used to the idea of us, but my inner wildcat wants to tell her immediately and doesn't understand why we're waiting to claim her."

"Tell her soon, and we can have another party here before you go back to tell your Redstone family," Arlo mused. "That's one thing about being part of this Pack. I really enjoy all the celebrations we've been having. It makes the Pack stronger and grounds those of us who haven't yet found our mates."

"Honestly, I never expected to find a mate, much less a woman like Sunny. I've had to change my mind about fate. If it's meant to be, it just happens, and all our thinking about it isn't going to change it. I believe there's someone out there for every one of us. We just have to be in the right place at the right time to find her," Den told his friend.

"I don't know. Some of us have been waiting an awful long time," Arlo replied, looking around at the happy people in the room. "Still, it's good to see others keeping our kind going strong. Being a wolf, it's all about the Pack for us. Is it that way for you?"

"To some extent. I mean, I was happy for my sister when she found her mate. Our mother was pressuring all of us about giving her grandchildren." Arlo guffawed at Den's disgusted tone.

Den laughed along with him, realizing only as he said the words that he didn't dislike the idea of having children as much as he had before. In fact, he loved the idea…if Sunny was their mom. But keeping in mind what he'd just said about fate, he would wait and see what happened. First, he had to get Sunny to agree to be his. After that, they could talk about children and whatever else life together might bring.

Den was gratified when Sunny sought him out as dinner was served. They sat next to each other at the table with the Alpha pairs. Conversation flowed, and they had a lovely meal before the music started up and most of the crowd started dancing.

Den waited for a slow song before asking Sunny to join him on the dance floor. It was a strategic move that ended with them dancing close for song after song, regardless of what the tempo of the next songs turned out to be. They were in their own little world, holding each other close and just enjoying the moment.

A little before eleven, Den and Sunny made their excuses and went upstairs to call her parents back. Den had received details of what Jason had arranged to get Sunny's folks to Wyoming and would be able to pass them on once her parents indicated they would accept Jason's invitation.

Sunny was relieved that her parents would be coming to Wyoming. She hadn't felt right about letting them go home to possible danger. This way, they could all be together, and her folks could meet her sister and cousin and the whole Pack. They'd made her feel so welcome tonight. She couldn't imagine a nicer party than the one she'd just enjoyed.

She chatted with her mother for a bit, telling her about the party and how nice everyone had been. Den gave her dad the flight details that Jason had set up. He also vouched personally for the pilot, intimating that they were old military colleagues and fellow cat shifters, though he claimed the pilot was a jaguar, not a mountain lion. He also cautioned them both against asking too many questions since most shifters wouldn't take kindly to too much curiosity about themselves.

He was gentle with them and kind. Sunny liked the way Den talked with her parents, as if they were already old and trusted friends. Her mother liked Den already, Sunny could tell. Her dad was thawing but holding a bit in reserve, which was typical of him. Sunny wanted them to get to know Den. They would love him as much as she did.

Wait. She stopped herself in wonder at her own thoughts. *Love?*

Sunny thought about that for a moment while Den passed on more details to her father for their flight. Did she love him? It didn't seem possible, but there was a definite section of her heart that already had his name on it. He'd been so good to her. So helpful and kind. He'd saved her life and brought her to her blood kin. He'd given her the most incredible ecstasy she'd ever experienced. He'd been just…great. Superlative in every way.

It seemed outrageous. She'd never fallen in love so fast or so deeply, but there it was. She loved Den. A little bit of doubt crept in. Could he possibly love her too? Would he ever? Or was this just a fling for him?

He'd seemed very serious about everything to this point, and her sister had told her that shifters didn't mess around with women's minds. If this was going to be a wham-bam sort of thing, he probably would have been up front with her about that from the beginning. But she didn't get that impression.

No, everything he'd said and done had made her feel he was looking to explore whatever might grow between them with an eye toward making a commitment, if that made sense long-term. She still wasn't exactly sure how shifters found their mates, but it was clear that they didn't always mate with other shifters. After all, both her sister and her cousin were mated to werewolves, and neither woman could shapeshift.

Sunny began to wonder how big cats thought about mating outside the shifter species. Would Den be open to keeping Sunny with him permanently? Could it be possible that they might be mates? She certainly hoped so. She loved the big galoot and found she wanted his love in return.

"We'll see you tomorrow afternoon, Sunny," her mother said, refocusing Sunny's attention to the ongoing video call.

"Okay, Mom. Have a safe flight, and I'll see you when you get here. Love you both!" Sunny signed off with her folks and shut down the laptop.

She felt tired but in a happy way. So much had happened today. It had been a truly great day.

Den took her hand and captured her attention. She turned to look at him. They were sitting side by side on the edge of the big bed.

"You had a big day. Are you all right?" he asked, his gaze searching hers.

"Just a little tired, but you're right. I was just thinking what a great day it's been. So much new information and such great people. I can't believe how much my life has changed in such a short time," she admitted.

"Do you want me to go to another room, or is sharing one room okay with you?" he asked, his voice dipping low and firing her senses. Suddenly, she wasn't really that tired anymore.

CHAPTER 17

"Oh, I think one room is more than enough for us," Sunny said, feeling a bit frisky. She placed her hands on his chest, enjoying the feel of his beating heart.

"Are you sure about this?" Den asked, moving in close. "I should warn you, my cat and me are getting pretty serious about you."

"Good," she said, daring even more. "I'm getting pretty serious about you too."

"You don't say?" His tone was all cat-with-the-cream suave and satisfied as he moved even closer.

He kissed her, taking her down to the bed so that he was over her. She was more than ready to surrender to his dominance. She knew by now that he would never ask more of her than she was willing to give and never push her too far outside her comfort zone, though he would encourage her to try new things that he thought she would like. So far, he hadn't been wrong.

His hands were everywhere, unbuttoning and unzipping, removing and tossing away. Her clothes were gone, and his followed in short order until they were both naked on the big bed. Just as she'd wanted.

She pushed at his shoulders, and they rolled until she was on top, and then, she sat back on her haunches, straddling him, grinning down at his handsome face. He gave her a sexy smile that nearly melted her bones, lifting his hands to cup her bare breasts.

"I like this position," he murmured.

"Mm," she said, squirming a bit as she sought the contact between her legs that she wanted. "I do too."

He wasn't quite inside her yet, but she was working her way up to that. She just wanted to enjoy the moment and give him a little bit of the delicious torment he'd been dishing out to her without even trying. All he had to do was look at her, and she remembered the way it felt to have him inside her. Just the memory of their time together made her blood flow hot and desire rage. She'd been thinking of being alone with him again for hours. Ever since the last time they'd been together, in fact.

And now, she had him where she'd wanted him, and they'd waited long enough. She readjusted her position and slid down onto him, taking him deep and full. Sweet heaven, he felt good!

Just like that, she felt complete. Not sated but fulfilled in some nebulous way she couldn't quite define. There was more, she knew. She looked forward to the pleasure she knew he would bring her.

Slowly, at first, she began to move in a steady rhythm, her head dropping back as the desire built inside her. Her mouth dropped open, and Den teased her breasts, rising slightly to lick and suck. He knew just how to drive her wild.

Climax hit her easily, and she lost her rhythm to spasms of delight that made her cry out his name. Den rolled them, so that he was in charge, and she was more than willing to let him have his way. She could trust him to keep this going until they were both well satisfied. She knew that already from their prior experience. Den had staying power and was the kind of man who could make her come multiple times before taking his own pleasure. She'd felt a little guilty about it, but he seemed to take pride in how many times he could make her say his name.

She would call it conceit, but he had a right to it, she thought with a satisfied grin. The man had talent. Or maybe they were just…totally compatible in a way she had never before experienced. Yeah, maybe that was it. Or maybe it was just that he owned her heart, soul, and body. Not that she'd told him that. She wasn't sure if she would ever reveal the depth of her feelings for him. So far, he hadn't spoken of emotions, and she wasn't sure if bringing them up would please him or send him running as far and fast as he could.

She really didn't think he was that kind of guy, but why take the chance? Not when she could have this kind of amazing pleasure. She wouldn't do anything to mess this up. Not yet. Not ever, if she could somehow manage that, but she knew their time together was going to be short, one way or another. Events were progressing outside this room that would necessitate their parting. Not that she wanted to part from him, but life might do it anyway. In fact, it probably would. But she wasn't going to think about that now.

No. Right now, she was going to enjoy every last moment of being with Den. She knew, deep in her heart, she would never have a better, more thoughtful, or talented lover. Den was in a class of his own, and she was going to savor this experience.

He took over, as she'd known he would, and began sliding in a rhythmic pattern that reignited her desire. Of course, her desire hadn't been very far beneath the surface to begin with. Being with Den had taught her things about her own body that she'd never known before. Like her newfound capacity for multiple orgasms in rapid succession that left her totally breathless with satisfaction. Only Den had ever brought that delight to her.

And here he was, doing it again. She came with a moan, and he built her right back up again, riding her through the ecstasy and into the next wave as if there was no beginning and no end. No him or her as separate entities. Only *them*. Together. One.

United in purpose. And their purpose at this moment was a passion the lit the sky with an aurora borealis of bliss. Their own private ethereal light show that only they could see in the privacy of their own shared desire.

Den changed positions after her next climax, rolling her to her tummy and lifting her hips into the air. She obliged him with lethargic movements. Her body was already humming with so much intensity she found it hard to concentrate. He chuckled in that almost smug masculine way that lit fires in her blood. She loved his mastery over her body and her passions. She loved everything about the way he made her feel. She was very much afraid...she loved...him.

Heart, soul, body, and mind. She was a goner, that was for sure. After knowing Den, she feared—and fully expected—she would never be the same again. Which, she discovered, she didn't really mind. Not when he gave her such mind-blowing orgasms to remember him by.

He slid back into her from behind, reaching a new spot within her that drove her even higher. She gave a short keening cry every time he thrust, unsure whether or not she would live through the next inevitable climax. She'd never felt this way before. Never so high. Never so intense. Heaven help her, she'd never felt so alive, even when she'd been dancing.

Sunny came with a primal sound ripped from the depths of her soul. It was raw and powerful, just like the way Den made her feel with every last pulse of him inside her. He came a moment later, tensing behind her and clutching her hips with almost bruising intensity.

When they had both wrung every last frisson of pleasure out of being together, Den removed himself from her body and then lay down behind her, spooning her body into his. She felt his warmth and his caring in every gesture. She felt...cherished, even if he'd never speak words of love.

A little pang ran through her heart at that thought, but she pushed it firmly aside. She was living for today. Enjoying the moment. Her car accident and incomplete recovery had taught her that living in the moment was really the only thing she could do. It was the only way to make sense of a usually nonsensical world. Firmly resolved, she would enjoy this time with Den while she could and not think about the future.

At least, not much. She couldn't stop her mind from wandering into forbidden areas occasionally, but she was on alert to push it right back over into the safe zone, should it do so. That was the only way to handle this situation without setting herself up for a really big fall when they went their separate ways. She was protecting herself. Wasn't she?

Then, why did the idea of parting from Den leave her feeling hollow? Damn.

After another few moments of heartbreaking uncertainty, she fell asleep cuddled in Den's arms. He woke her sometime later, his cock already inside her from behind. He hadn't really had to move her body much at all to slip inside. He'd just done it, and the presumption made her gasp as she came fully awake.

"I hope you don't mind," he whispered in her ear from behind, nipping at the lobe playfully. "I thought waking you with a kiss was too cliché." His wry chuckle set her senses on fire.

"So, you decided to wake me with a…" She wanted to say the word, but it felt scandalous.

"Wake you with a fuck?" he completed the thought, sending a zing of excitement through her body and straight to her core, where they were joined. He licked her neck then bit down slightly, not bruising but enticing. He slid deeper inside her as she bent a bit to accommodate their position. "How do you like it?"

She gasped as he pushed deeper with every long stroke.

"I want to be upset with you, but I can't bring myself to regret anything," she admitted, gasping out the words as he pushed her into an orgasm that seemed to go on and on as he

BIANCA D'ARC

kept thrusting, shallow now, not really leaving her for long, as if he couldn't stand not being inside her as deeply as he could get. She was all for that. Especially when it felt so delicious.

She came and came while he chuckled darkly and nibbled on her earlobe and neck. Then, after a long while, he was all business, thrusting hard and deep, positioning her as if she were a doll, all to achieve better depth and penetration. She did whatever he wanted, trusting him to know what was best. And boy-o-boy, it really was the best. The best she'd ever had. Ever.

She came, and then, he did, riding her throughout as their bodies tensed and shuddered. He said her name in the most enticing growl while she moaned and gasped, gripped by the most intense feelings she'd ever experienced. Den just kept showing her new heights. One thing was for certain—being with Den was never just average. Every time they fucked—to use his excitingly crude word—it got better and better.

Later, as they lazed in bed in the middle of the night, Sunny spoke, musing aloud. Her hand rubbed absently over his chest, enjoying the feel of his rough chest hair against her palm and the hard muscles beneath his skin.

"You know, my parents will be here tomorrow," she began hesitantly. "I don't want this to end, but…"

"It doesn't have to," he offered in a low voice.

"I can't… Not with my parents here," she objected.

"What if I asked your father for your hand in marriage? That's how humans do it, right?" Den asked, seemingly totally serious. She gazed up at him, almost holding her breath.

"Are you asking me to marry you?"

"Actually, I was hoping you would accept me as your mate. Among shifters, that's like marriage, only permanent. Mates are forever. There's no such thing as divorce among my kind. Once mated, we are completely loyal and devoted," he told her, meeting her gaze. "Sunny, you are my mate. I just need for you to agree, and we'll be married in the eyes of my people. I'd be happy to have a human-style ceremony, if that's your wish, but in my heart, I am already your husband." He sounded so serious.

"Why?" she asked, needing just one more thing to make her happiness complete.

"Because I love you."

There it was. The thing she needed most in the world and hadn't really dared hope for. His love.

"Well, thank heaven for that!" She breathed a sigh of relief. "I love you too, Den. So much. It was just about making me crazy, wondering if you felt the same. I kept telling myself not to expect anything, to just enjoy the moment, but I was fooling myself."

"Sorry. I didn't want to scare you off, so I was being cautious. My inner cat kept pushing me to pounce on you and get you to accept us. You do accept me, don't you? I kind of need to hear the words." He chuckled, a guarded sort of joy dawning over his handsome features. She crawled upward to place kisses on his jaw, his cheeks, his lips. Talking as she kissed him, her happiness knowing no bounds.

"Let's be clear. Yes, I'll be your mate, and yes, you should probably talk to my dad, if you want to start your relationship with my parents on the right foot, and yes, we're going to have a wedding. Maybe on the ranch, if and when it's safe again." Her joy bubbled over as she straddled him and began a new round of lovemaking that lasted into the next morning.

They did get a little bit of sleep here and there, but mostly, they spent the night indulging in their love for one another and the joy of being together. Sunny was so amazed by the way Den made her feel. To think that he would be her mate...forever... It boggled the mind. He wasn't going to leave her when times got tough. Not like her last boyfriend. Den was going to be there for her through thick and thin, as she would be for him. Because they loved each other and shared a mutual respect. How did she ever get so blessed?

The next morning, they were both tired, but happy. Those at breakfast realized that something had changed between them, and it wasn't long before the news spread among the Pack that their new member, Sunny, had mated with the werecougar.

CHAPTER 18

Den held back as Sunny's parents got out of the vehicle that had met them at the airstrip. Arlo was driving, and he signaled to Den as three others got out of the SUV. Sunny's parents and another man Den knew from the service. The jaguar shifter pilot named Hank nodded to Den and walked over to say hello to Jesse and Jason, who stood off to one side.

Sunny was introducing her folks to Sally and Maria, so Den sidled over to where the guys were standing a few yards distant. Jason had welcomed Hank to Pack lands, and Jesse was chatting with him, congratulating Hank on his mating. Den arrived in time to add his congratulations to Jesse's and receive Hank's in return.

"What do you think of your passengers?" Jesse asked the pilot.

"Nice people. Very gentle spirits. They were at an art retreat, at least, that's what they were calling it. Roderigo told me the retreat had a separate, hidden component that was really a gathering of low-ranked mages. Artists, craftspeople, and people who create things that are imbued with their magic. Rody is looking into it a bit further for the Clan, which is why he was one of the instructors, and Nick said he'll copy Jesse on the report once it's fully compiled."

"Thanks," Jesse said at once.

They all knew the "Nick" Hank was referring to was the incredibly well-connected second-in-command of the small-but-mighty jaguar Clan headed by eccentric billionaire Mark Pepard. They had all sorts of information sources not available to the common man…or shifter.

"Thing is," Hank went on, "some of those people make very powerful items that might be useful in our fight against the Destroyer. Mark is considering funding a few of them to make stuff for us. He said he'd be happy to talk to you, if you want to discuss it further. Especially seeing as how you have an in with the family of one of the more prominent artisan-mages. Apparently, Sunny's folks are big in that community, and their ranch is rumored to be both a refuge for others like them and a training ground. They're both well-respected mage teachers to those with gifts like their own."

Den was fascinated by all that Hank and his Clan had been able to find out in such a short time. Someone must have been working on this late last night, getting the details from Roderigo that would have otherwise waited until he'd gone back home to Jaguar Island.

"Thanks for bringing them here and for your work on this, Hank. Please pass along my regards to those of your Clan that helped, especially Rody. I owe you all one," Den said quietly.

They were both big cat shifters, even if they were from different species. They understood one another a little better than they understood the wolves. Cats were likely to be way more independent and even a bit aloof. If a few jaguars had gone out of their way, it was definitely worth remarking on and thanking them publicly. Couldn't get much more public than in front of two strong wolf Alphas like Jesse and Jason.

They didn't have a chance to say anything more as Sunny

brought her folks over to meet the men. Hank took a step back while Sally took over, introducing Jason, then Maria introduced Jesse, and finally, Sunny beamed as she brought them around to Den.

Den shook hands with Sunny's dad, knowing he was being evaluated and sized up. Sunny's mom gave Den a hug and told him to call her Marilisa.

It was some time later, when they were sitting around a table in the common room of the Pack house, enjoying coffee and snacks, that they got down to business. The two Alpha couples were present, as were Sunny's folks, Hank, Sunny, and Den. A big platter of baked goodies had been left at the center of the table along with insulated pots of coffee, tea and bottles of water.

Sunny's parents had asked everyone to call them by their first names. They seemed exactly as advertised—quiet people who kept to themselves but loved their adopted daughter very, very much.

"We always suspected Sunny had a lot of magic, but we didn't know what kind," Marilisa explained. "I knew we had to adopt her, though, to protect her. We weren't looking to adopt a child, but she ran up to me when I was walking from my car into a store one day, and I caught her before she got run over. She was just a tiny thing and had escaped the woman who'd been fostering her. We got to talking, and I realized Sunny needed someone who understood magic, because even as little as she was, she made my senses tingle with energy." Marilisa reached for Sunny's hand and squeezed it on the tabletop, smiling at her daughter. "I told Herman about her, and we applied to adopt the very next day."

"We watched over her as she grew, but her magic never really manifested in a way we could understand. She could make flowers bloom from a young age, but that was about all," Herman picked up the tale. "We didn't want to push her as we'd been pushed by our families. We didn't want to pressure her, but wanted to let her grow into whatever she

149

might become in her own good time. We didn't realize she had dryad blood. Frankly, that's something that never crossed our minds."

"It's not all that common," Sally said not unkindly. "I didn't know what I was until just recently, though I always had a way with houseplants."

"Me too," Maria put in. "Until I met Jesse, and he told me about my heritage, I had no idea."

"Thanks," Marilisa said sincerely. "To be honest, I feel like a fool now for not realizing or even thinking in that direction. To think of all the wasted time, when she could have known what she was or sought training from someone with more knowledge of what she could do. I'm sorry, honey," she said, turning to meet Sunny's eyes.

"There's nothing to be sorry for," Sunny insisted. "I think this has all played out as it was meant to be. Though I do wish I'd realized you were running a magic school at the ranch."

"It wasn't really that organized," Herman admitted. "We took in the occasional student who needed help or a place to decompress. There's a lot of pressure put on the children of certain magical lineages. Both Marilisa and I were disappointments to our families and wasted a lot of years trying to be something we weren't to please them. When we finally found each other, we went our own way and were promptly disowned by both our families."

"That's terrible," Maria said, compassion clear in her voice.

Marilisa sighed. "That's the way of magical families sometimes. There's a lot of pressure to perform and prove your worth. My family saw me as a disappointment because my magic expresses through my art. I always thought Sunny's might be expressed through her dancing, but though I saw hints of that from time to time, it never really manifested. At least, not on stage."

"Only when I danced among the trees," Sunny put in. "That's when my magic came closest to the surface," she agreed.

"I really must thank you, Maria, for helping Sunny with your healing skill. She's moving so much better already," Marilisa gushed, tears in her sparkling blue eyes. "I've been trying to make contact with a mage-healer for a long time, but since our families disowned us, the few I know of wouldn't speak to me."

"You were?" Sunny asked her mom. "I had no idea."

"I would do anything for you, sweetheart," Marilisa replied with love shining in her eyes. "You know that."

"I do. And I feel the same," Sunny replied with a watery smile as she leaned in and kissed her adoptive mother's cheek.

"I'm so grateful Sunny had you in her life, Marilisa," Sally said softly, watching them. "And you, Herman. I hope you don't mind that I asked Den to find her for me. My goal is not to intrude on your family, but to reconnect with mine and help our ancestor."

"Mind?" Herman asked, his tone incredulous. "How can we mind? You're our Sunny's flesh and blood. Of course, you needed to reconnect." Herman was taking it well, if Den was any judge.

In the momentary silence that fell after that statement, Jason changed the subject. They had even more serious matters to discuss and it was best to get that stuff out of the way.

"I spoke to Den's Clan mate, Brian, a short while ago," Jason reported. "There's been some damage done to your property. One of the barns on your ranch was broken into, apparently. Brian did a bit of reconnaissance, and the damage didn't look too bad, but I suggest you stay here for a few days. I also talked to the Redstone Alpha, and he's agreed to help with a strike team. Jesse?" Jason gestured for his brother to take up what was turning into a briefing.

"I'm hoping to send a small unit to Sacramento, with your permission, to capture or kill those who attacked your home," Jesse stated succinctly. Herman and Marilisa looked concerned and a bit shocked. "Have you ever heard of the Wraiths?" Jesse asked shortly, searching their faces.

"A legend, I thought," Herman replied, shaking his head. "Shifter mercenaries is the rumor."

"Yes," Jesse nodded in confirmation. "That's exactly what we are, but with one caveat. Most mercs work for the highest bidder. We only work for those on the side of Light. It's our guiding purpose."

"You mean to tell me that you're the Wraiths?" Herman looked from Jesse to Jason and back again.

"Not me," Jason said, smiling and holding up his hands, palms outward. "That's my brother's deal, and he does it very well. So well, in fact, that he's gathered a group of like-minded ex-military shifters around him. *Those* are the Wraiths."

"You *lead* the Wraiths?" Herman asked, nonplussed, looking at Jesse with a sort of awe-filled respect.

"I do," Jesse confirmed, "but I hope you'll keep that to yourself. Of course, as events are unfolding, I think the time for secrecy is nearly at an end. Our side is going to need every asset at its disposal if we're going to stop the Destroyer."

Now, Herman and Marilisa looked fearful and disbelieving.

"Do you have information that she's really back?" Marilisa asked in a near-whisper.

"Nothing solid as yet, but it's looking more and more like she returned to our realm a while back and is regaining her energy. From everything I've been told, moving between dimensions like that—especially from the farthest realm to this one—takes a lot out of you." Jesse shook his head. "I'm preparing because I think we'll all be called upon to act in concert sooner rather than later, and it's better to be prepared and not be called upon than need to act and not be ready."

"I can agree with that," Herman muttered, nodding. "What do you plan to do on our ranch?" he asked a moment later.

"Small strike team with local Redstone support. We go in,

assess the damage done, try to disarm any traps that might have been laid, and make the place safe for some specialist support to go in and decontaminate anything that might have been magically tainted. We know the *Venifucus* use blood magic rather routinely, and I probably don't have to tell you how that fouls everything it touches." Jesse outlined the plan. "I'd like to lay a trap with an eye toward ending the immediate threat. The only problem I foresee on an ongoing basis is that, if one group of *Venifucus* operatives know about your place, I have little doubt others do now too."

"We can't go home?" Marilisa sounded aghast, and Herman put his arm around her shoulders.

"After we finish clearing it out, yes, you can, but it may not be safe long-term," Jesse clarified. "I wish I could tell you otherwise, but I think it's best to be honest."

"Of course," Jason added, "you are welcome to stay here with us until Jesse's team is done. You might find you like the area and want to resettle someplace close by. I know Sally is hoping to talk her sister into a long visit, at the very least. Maybe you'd like to stay in the area as well. But you can think about that as long as you need to. Right now, I think Jesse just needs your permission to send his strike team onto your property."

"By all means," Herman said, "if you can help stop the evil, then that's the right thing to do." He looked down, his brows drawing together in thought before he continued. "I'm not sure how much I can pay you for your assistance…"

Jesse held up his hands, palms outward. "No charge, sir. You're family now." The smile on his face widened as he looked at his mate then at Sunny.

"I'm not quite sure that's exactly how mercenaries work," Herman quipped, chuckling. "But I appreciate the assistance. Perhaps there's something we can do for you in return. Our magic may be quite benign, but we do pretty good glyphs of protection, talismans, and wards."

Den spoke up. "The wards around the property were very high quality. They let me in, but not the bad guys, and it took the enemy agents a great deal of time, work, and energy to get through them."

Jesse nodded then smiled at Herman. "That's very generous of you. Thanks." He stood, pushing back his chair. "But if you'll excuse me, I'm just going to send the strike team on its way. The sooner we do this the less damage the enemy has time to do on your property." He left the table, gesturing to a few men who had been sitting or standing elsewhere in the large room, and left with them.

"We're probably going to have to relocate," Herman said finally, speaking into the silence after Jesse's departure. "Our ranch was a safe haven, not only for us, but for others like us who have a hard time fitting in with the expectations of most of the older magical families. We are artists, but we are also teachers. Our school of magic is not exactly revered among the others. We don't teach combat. We don't teach offensive things or, really, defensive things either, though many of our creations do contain protective magic. We basically teach art, in many different forms. Not the technique, necessarily, but the way to imbue whatever art you excel at with magic. Like I said, it's not exactly a high priority for most mage schools." He chuckled wryly.

"What my husband is trying to say is that we don't get a lot of respect from other magic users. For the most part, we're okay with that. We went our own way a long time ago, and it's been good for us, but there are a lot of younger mages with the same issue who struggle. Those are the ones that come to us for guidance and acceptance," Marilisa explained. "We need a safe place for them and for us. If our ranch is no longer a closely held secret, then we're going to have to find another place to continue our work."

Jason's expression turned thoughtful. "I may have an idea about a place that could use some looking after, but I'll have to make a few calls. In the meantime, you're more than welcome to stay here as long as you need to. Either in the Pack house, or if you think you'll be more comfortable somewhere else, we can help you find a place of your own nearby."

"For now, we'll accept your gracious offer to stay here," Herman said with a respectful nod to Jason. "We are very grateful. I don't know what we would've done otherwise. Thank you, Alpha."

CHAPTER 19

While her folks were settling in to the suite of rooms they'd been assigned in the Pack house and Den was off with Jesse and Jason talking about military stuff, Sally pulled Sunny aside. They went out on the back deck, Maria with them, and sat.

"I want to show you something," Sally said, leaning forward in her seat.

She held her hand out, palm down and closed her eyes. Within moments, an image shimmered into being. It was a tree. Its tip was at Sally's palm and its trunk went down to the floor of the deck. There were many branches reaching out in a conical configuration, with people's images on them. Sally opened her eyes.

"This is our family tree," Sally said, looking at the shimmering golden tree that wasn't solid at all, but a thing made of magic that would dissipate as soon as she released the magic holding it together.

"That's amazing!" Sunny said, squinting to look at some of the branches.

"Mine looks mostly the same but has a few different branches and the color is more greenish-gold," Maria offered, looking at the twinkling magical tree.

"Can I learn how to do that?" Sunny asked, her voice a low whisper.

Sally grinned at her and let the magic dissipate. "Yes. That's why I brought you out here. I thought maybe you'd want to try it out a few times away from the crowd. It took me a while to get comfortable with calling it."

"Me too," Maria laughed. "Sally showed me, but I couldn't get the hang of it at first. I had to practice a lot until I got comfortable."

Forewarned by that exchange, Sunny expected it to be harder than it was. She was surprised when she turned out to be rather a quick study. Within just a few attempts, Sunny was able to produce a shimmering golden-brown tree as complex as Sally's. Since they were sisters, their tree was the same, except for the color. Sally's was more gold, where Sunny's was a shade darker.

Sunny was able to rotate the tree so she could see it from all angles. There was something about one of the branches that called to her. She leaned in to look and was hit by a *knowing*. She couldn't explain it any other way. She just suddenly knew that was the next person they had to contact.

"This one," she said, hardly aware of what she was saying. "We're going to find her next. She's already on her way."

Sunny released the magic and slumped back in her chair. Something had just happened, but she really wasn't sure what it was. She just...knew. That branch. That distant relative. That was the one that would arrive next.

"Has that ever happened to you before?" Sally asked quietly.

When Sunny looked over at her sister, Sally was eyeing her strangely. Sunny took a deep breath and realized she felt drained somehow. Suddenly tired, as if she'd expended a lot of energy. Perhaps she had. She really wasn't all that familiar with this sort of magic and had never consciously used it before. She wasn't really sure what she was capable of or what it might do to her. She shook her head.

"Never," she replied. "Of course, I've never manifested a glowing tree before either. This has been a day of firsts, for sure."

"Her name is Crystal," Maria put in. "I sensed it before you let the tree go."

"I guess we need to prepare or something," Sally said, still looking tentative. She turned her gaze back on Sunny. "You've never been clairvoyant or anything, have you?"

"Not that I know of," Sunny replied at once. "I guess we can ask my folks, to be certain. If anyone would know, they would."

"I think we should do that," Sally said, seeming to think out loud. "And I guess you should also be on the lookout for any further manifestations of clairvoyance. I'll have to ask those with more knowledge of magic than I have, but it could be that your power is different than mine, even though we're sisters."

"The color of her tree is different," Maria observed. "As is mine. It makes sense that each of us will have the dryad power to different extents and in different areas. I just never thought seeing the future was something a dryad could do."

"We'll have to do more research," Sally said finally, seeming more comfortable with the idea now that they'd talked it over. "Jason's got some connections I can call on. The High Priestess has been a wealth of information. I bet she would know. At the very least, she could set us on the right path." Sally nodded almost to herself. "I'm going to give her a call tomorrow."

When Sunny and Den reunited about an hour later, she told him all about the weird events on the back deck. He didn't seem as concerned about her moment of what might have been foresight as she was.

"You're new to using your abilities," he told her. "There are bound to be some surprises along the way. Did you get a sense of where this Crystal woman might be found?"

She shook her head. "I didn't get the feeling she was going to roll up the driveway and knock on the Pack house door. I think she's going to be found by an ally and be put in touch with us that way. I can't say exactly why I feel that way, but I think that's what might happen."

Den nodded slowly. "Okay then. We'll wait and see, and if that is what happens, then we'll have more data about your abilities. Maybe you should start to keep a journal or something so we can keep track. If you do have the power of foresight, then that could be really useful in the future."

"So, you don't think it's weird?" She had to be sure. She'd never dealt with anything like this before.

"Not at all." He was quick to reassure her. "Foresight is a gift that some people have to greater or lesser extents. It's a super useful thing that should be cultivated if you do turn out to have it. Either way, it's interesting that you had such a strong reaction to your first taste of real magic. And, from what you said, calling up the tree came relatively easy to you. That has to mean that you're much more magical than you know."

"Huh." She hadn't thought about that. "You're right. Maria said she really struggled to bring forth the tree at first. She does it easily now, but it was really hard for her in the beginning."

"And you found it easy," he reminded her. "You said as much when you told me about what you gals had gotten up to while I was talking strategy with the guys."

Sunny was nodding. "You're right." She thought about how her small uses of magic had occurred in years past. "I used to have to dance to make things bloom. After the accident, I learned how to do it with less movement and less *precise* movements. But I wasn't moving at all today. We were seated on the deck, and I was able to just call on the magic once Sally explained how."

They were sitting in a quiet corner of the common room. People were bustling about, preparing the next meal that would be served buffet style at the other end of the large room.

"I talked to your father earlier," Den told her, changing the subject and stealing her breath. "I explained to him how things stood between us and asked very formally for your hand in marriage. I thought he was going to punch me in the nose at first, but then, he calmed down, and we had a really good, open, frank conversation. He really loves you, princess." Den smiled softly and looked deep into her eyes. "I'm glad you have parents who care that deeply about you. I want you to know that our mating doesn't have to change your relationship with them too much. We can move to wherever you want. I was already contemplating—more than contemplating, actually—leaving my birth Clan to join the Wraiths, but Jesse and Jason both understand that mating changes everything. I'll go anywhere and do anything you want to do. If you want to live near your folks, that's fine with me. I want you to know that."

Sunny was flabbergasted. She had thought Den's joining the Wraiths was more or less a done deal. She'd figured he was going to live on this mountain and work with Jesse and his guys. She hadn't really thought about where that would leave her, just yet. There was too much going on. Too many variables to consider. Her sister was here. Her cousin, Maria, was here. Sunny wanted to get to know both of them better. And, of course, she wanted to be with Den. Wherever he was, that's where she wanted to be.

But her parents... She wanted to make sure they were okay too. The ranch was still a problem. It might not be safe to go back there. If so, she didn't know where they were going to end up and how that would affect her. She wanted to be near them, but she also wanted to be with Den. It was a problem she couldn't work out in the next few minutes, or even the next few days.

But Den had just given her a gift. He would do more than compromise. He would do whatever was best for her. Of course, she wanted to do what was right for him too. She'd have to think very seriously about their next moves.

She leaned forward and kissed him, then drew back. "I love that you're so willing to put aside your own aspirations for my comfort, but I can't answer right now where we're going to end up. We need to figure out where my folks are going to be, and I do want to spend time with my sister and cousin. For now, let's see if maybe we can just stay here for a while, and then, perhaps in time, the more permanent solution will come clear."

"Fair enough," Den said at once. "For the record, your dad gave his permission, so it looks like we're getting hitched." He grinned at her, and she had to laugh.

Later that night, after another great meal with the Pack and her parents, Den and Sunny went to their room. It was in a different part of the Pack house than the suite to which Sunny's folks had been assigned.

Den took Sunny into his arms and carried her to the bed, kissing her even before he set her down. He placed her on the bed and followed her down, covering her willing body with his, surrounding her with his warmth, passion, and love.

"I'm so glad I found you, princess," Den whispered as he drew back, shucking his clothes as quickly as he could.

"I'm glad too," she told him, pulling off her own clothing in a frenzy of need.

They were perfectly in sync and desperate to be together as one, but Den stilled her movements, one of his large hands reaching out to cup her cheek. He looked deep into her eyes and time stood still.

"I love you with everything I am, Sunny. My heart, my soul, my wild spirit. It's all for you."

Sunny caught her breath. He was so serious. His words so incredibly profound. The moment stretched.

"I love you the same way, Den. Everything in me wants to be with you. Forever and always. As long as we live," she whispered back and felt satisfaction as his eyes swirled with the wildcat magic of his inner beast. The cat seemed to like her words as much as his human side did.

"Then, that's exactly what we'll do," Den said quietly. "We'll live happily ever after." His grin made her laugh.

"I like the sound of that!"

EPILOGUE

Two months later, in Sacramento…

Sunny was thrilled to be back on stage at the ballet company she had thought to never see again after her accident. She was performing a special solo at a gala put on to raise money for the local hospital. Those doctors and nurses had been so good to her. They'd done the best they could with non-magical resources to help her walk again. They had called her a medical miracle, but the real miracle had been performed by her magical cousin, Maria.

When Sunny had visited her old friend Paulina and the dance studio owner realized how much better Sunny was than the last time they'd seen each other, Paulina had devised this plan. A triumphant return—for one night only—of the prima ballerina who had suffered so greatly, then benefited from the hospital's good work. It was a perfect angle to raise what they hoped would be record-setting numbers of donations for the hospital, and a great way to publicize the ballet company, as well. A win-win.

Sunny had agreed, but only because she loved to dance and needed to prove to herself that she was fully healed. She would never tour with a ballet company again, but she had to know that she could, if she'd wanted to. It was an important step to putting the horror of the accident and the painful months of recovery behind her.

She also wanted to dance for Den. She wanted him to see her as she had been, not as the broken wreck of a woman he'd first met. He'd told her over and over that she was beautiful to him no matter what, but she felt the need to show him what she could really do, under the best possible conditions in a real theatre with bright lights and full orchestra.

She wanted him to know what her life had been like as a prima ballerina. She wanted him to fully understand her past so they could walk together, into the future.

The opportunity had been too good to pass up when Paulina had come up with this plan. Sunny and Den had come back to Sacramento with her folks, to help with the move. After they packed up all their stuff, all of them were going back to Wyoming, for the time being.

Sunny's parents would retain ownership of the ranch property, but the Redstones were going to use it as a base and keep any potential bad guys away for the foreseeable future. This way, her folks wouldn't have to rush into any big decisions. They could live in Wyoming for a while before they figured out where they were going to settle, but they'd had to come back to supervise the packing of all their belongings—and especially their studios, supplies, and artwork.

Den had been helping, as had the Redstone crew, especially Den's sister, who had really hit it off with Sunny's mother. The two of them were off and running, trying to plan every last detail of the human-style wedding Sunny and Den were going to have next summer. Sunny was content to let her mother have her way with the wedding planning, while

Sunny spent her days preparing for her performance. She used Paulina's dance studio to rehearse and didn't let Den see what she was up to. She wanted it to be a surprise.

And so, she had brought him to the ballet gala, then left him sitting with his sister and her husband, plus a few other members of their crew who had wanted to come. Sunny had gone backstage to prepare for her triumphant return to the stage and her official last appearance.

She was scheduled to go on later in the program, as a special guest of the company. Basically, her story was the star attraction that night and she was sure the celebrity announcer was going to milk it for all it was worth. She didn't mind. As long as her story could help this worthy cause, she didn't mind being the topic of the evening.

The hustle and bustle of backstage was familiar. She had missed this. She saw many dancers she had known from her past work with the company. She greeted the woman who had taken her place as a principal dancer with a hug and heartfelt congratulations. Sunny was no longer bitter about having lost her place after the wreck. Everything that had happened to her had led her to a really great place. Although she could have done without the injury and pain, she consoled herself with the knowledge that her life was so much richer now with Den and her extended family.

The corps de ballet was in near-constant motion as the show proceeded. Sunny found the dressing room she was sharing with her replacement and got into her costume with the help of the dresser. She put on her stage makeup and pulled her hair back into its tight ballerina bun, stabbing it into place with a multitude of hairpins to make sure it wouldn't come loose no matter what.

Then, she put on her toe shoes and started warming up. She would be on soon and she had timed it just right so that she'd be ready to go just in time for her big solo performance. Someone tapped on the door and gave her the five-minute warning. Sunny took a deep breath and headed out. She would be the consummate professional, as she always had been. She'd be ready to go the moment her cue came up.

She heard the tail end of the emcee's introduction but shunted it from her mind. She knew the story of her accident was being told and the doctors who had treated her were being named and congratulated. She didn't need to hear that. Not when she had to focus on the dance. She sent herself into that zone where nothing mattered but the movement and the music. And then…she danced out onto the stage as the music began.

Exhilaration was a pale word for what she felt as the dance progressed. She was elated. Inspired. Humbled and so incredibly happy. For the first time in over a year, she was able to dance, in public, on a real stage, with an orchestra and lighting and the magic that was the theater. She danced her heart out. She danced for herself. She danced for her mate. She danced for the sake of dance and felt her magic ignite in a way it never had before, but it wasn't anything dangerous or showy. It just was her soul, expressed through movement.

She had choreographed a short piece that told the story of her dancing, her accident, her heartache and pain at not being able to dance, and then her difficult recovery, as she regained the ability to move, bit by bit. Her struggle brought tears to many eyes in that audience and her magic expressed itself through her movement, touching all who saw her dance. They would never know it, but they would remember the dance that explained everything about the last tumultuous year of Sunny's life and the joy she felt now that she had found the love of her life.

When she finished her choreography and the music ended, she felt the hush of the audience in the moment before they burst into thunderous applause. She looked out over the footlights and saw more than a few people reaching up to wipe away tears. Sunny eased out of her final pose and curtsied low, accepting the applause as graciously as she could. Her eyes sought out Den, sitting at the front of the theater. He was standing, as was everyone else, clapping along with the crowd, the love shining out of his eyes.

There. He understood. He had now seen and understood the her that she had once been. That's why she had done this. That, and for the hospital, which was trying to raise funds to build a special pediatric unit.

Sunny accepted the standing ovation and the giant bouquet of roses that someone brought out to her. She bowed low, happy now that she had done this. She had achieved closure and was leaving her career at a high point, on her terms. No regrets.

She took one final bow and left the stage. There were a few more speeches and pleas for donations before a final group dance number that would put all of the current stars of the ballet on the stage together for the final performance of the evening. Sunny didn't want to be part of that. They'd asked, but she'd politely declined. She went back to the dressing room to change. She wanted to be ready when the show ended so she could go back to Den and really start her new life, leaving this old part of her behind.

Every step she took now brought her closer to her future with Den, in whatever form that was going to take. They were going to visit his family in Las Vegas so everybody could meet her and have another mating party. Then, they were going to have a real wedding next summer, giving her mother enough time to make plans. They still needed to figure out where they were going to live, but her folks were going to Wyoming, so she and Den would start there. That would give Sunny time to really get to know her sister and cousin. The rest, they would figure out as they went along. She wasn't too worried about it. She was happy as long as she was with Den, wherever they happened to wind up.

Den went backstage with an armful of flowers for Sunny. His mate was amazing, but of course, he had already known that. He hadn't truly understood why this had been so important to her until he'd seen her dance. The moment she stepped out onto the stage, he'd been transfixed. This beautiful, powerful, graceful woman was his mate, but she was more. More than he'd realized. She'd wanted him to see her as she had been and now he understood.

If she wanted to go back to performing, he'd follow her like a puppy—or, in his case, a housecat. All he wanted was for her to be happy, even if it meant he'd live the life of a stage husband. He didn't mind. Wherever she was, that's where he would be. Always.

He went backstage to congratulate her before the show ended. He'd come to see her performance. The rest didn't really matter to him.

Den wanted to lift her off her feet and carry her away to their bed so he could show her without words just how beautiful he thought she was. For now, though, he'd have to continue to share her with the people who wanted to meet her after that amazing performance. There was an after-party that they'd been invited to attend and since the charity was one she wanted to support, she had agreed to go.

His family was going too. His sister was in seventh heaven, hobnobbing with the elite of Sacramento society and evangelizing about Redstone Construction and their ethical standards and plans for the downtown renovations that were nearing completion. That was Diane—never passing up an opportunity to drum up more business for the firm, or just to spread goodwill.

Den knocked on the dressing room door and entered when Sunny called out. She was just fixing her earing when he walked in and caught her eye in the lighted mirror. She jumped up from her chair and went to him, all smiles.

"You were amazing, Sunny," he told her, handing her the flowers. She launched herself at him and he caught her around the waist, drawing her close for a quick kiss.

When she drew back her eyes were dazzling, her gaze filled with joy. He liked that look on her face and wanted to see it every day. He would make that his mission.

"I'm so glad I did this," she told him, collecting her things and then putting her arm through his.

The show was wrapping up, but they would leave early

and get to the party in time for Sunny to be on the receiving line with the other stars of the evening, including the top doctors from the hospital and the director of the ballet.

"Do you want to go back to performing?" he asked as they left the dressing room.

Sunny shook her head. "No, not really. It was never about the audience or adulation. It was all about the music and the dance. Having a live orchestra to dance to is a pretty heady feeling, and the lighting and costumes... It's really fun, but that part of my life is over now. I have new adventures awaiting. New adventures with you, Den." She squeezed his arm and pressed against his side for a moment. He loved what she had just said.

"I feel the same, you know," he replied in a low voice, just for her ears.

"I know," she fairly purred back at him.

They were inches away from kissing when the show ended and everyone came off the stage, heading for the dressing rooms. A male dancer stopped short, and Sunny looked up to see Alphonse—her ex-boyfriend who had dumped her after her accident. She had seen him in passing earlier, but they hadn't spoken. It looked like there would be no avoiding it now, though. Much as she'd prefer to just leave him securely in the past.

Maybe, though, she decided in a split second, this was also part of saying goodbye to dancing in the company, and the past. She decided to talk to him. He was insignificant to her now except as a memory. Talking to him would reinforce that new reality.

"Hello, Alphonse," Sunny said coolly. "You danced very well tonight."

"Sunny," he said, his voice even higher in pitch than she'd remembered. He had a sweet tenor singing voice. Though he was much more gifted as a dancer than a singer, he had enjoyed singing along with the radio and in the shower. After hearing Den's low rumble and purr for the past weeks, Alphonse's voice had lost any charm she'd ever thought it'd had. He seemed to be at a loss for words, looking at her and then at Den. "You're looking well," he said finally.

No thanks to him, she thought. He'd abandoned her faster than lightning when he'd realized she would never dance again. He was just that shallow. A real man would have stood by her and helped her recover. If Alphonse had cared at all for her, he never would have left her at that point in her life. She couldn't imagine Den doing something that hurtful to anyone. But Alphonse's abandonment had made her stronger in the end, though it had really sucked at the time.

"Thanks. It took time, but I'm back to normal now," she replied, smiling just a little. "This is my fiancé, Captain Dennis Palmer. He's just retired from the Army. He was a Green Beret." She turned to Den and gave him a dazzling smile. Darnit, she was enjoying this a little too much.

Putting Den side-by-side with Alphonse, there was just no comparison. She'd thought Alphonse had been hot. He was lean and muscular, but Den... Den was wild and tough and highly skilled in so many ways. Den was a Man with a capital Mmm. Alphonse was all show. Den was substance...and then some.

Damn. It was good to see this and realize that what she'd had in the past was nothing on what she had gained in the present. Den was a man to spend the rest of her life with. Alphonse had been a fun distraction for a while, but ultimately, he'd had no staying power.

"Nice to meet you," Alphonse muttered to Den as the two men shook hands. Den said little, simply giving Alphonse a measuring glance that seemed to make the dancer wither.

"Well, we're going to be late for the party. Maybe we'll see you there. If not, have a good life, Alphonse," she told him, sincerely.

"You too, Sunny," he said, refocusing on her. "I'm sorry for everything, and I'm glad you're okay now. You still have quite a gift. I watched your solo. You were poetry in motion."

Surprised by his compliment, she felt mildly pleased. At least they could part as friends. Something snicked into place in her heart, and she realized that last little broken piece had just clicked back into place. She was totally over Alphonse and now her entire heart belonged to Den. As it should be. They walked out arm in arm and headed for the party. She didn't speak to Alphonse again and didn't care. She'd received a closure she hadn't known she'd needed and enjoyed being on Den's arm as he made conversation—and a hefty contribution to the hospital fund.

"Den, are you rich or something?" she asked him privately as they stood on the balcony a bit later, getting a breath of fresh air.

"Well, I am part of the Redstone family, not just the Clan. My grandmother was a Redstone, actually. The family money comes down from her side, though none of my ancestors were what you might call poor."

"You're kidding." She rounded on him. "You mean I'm marrying a man of means and I didn't even realize it?"

He wrapped his hands around her waist and met her gaze, a smile playing around his lips. "I've got enough to keep you in any style you'd like, actually. My net worth is somewhere in the twenty million range, last time I checked, but I like to live simply."

Her jaw dropped. She'd had no clue he was that wealthy. Not that it mattered. She loved him. She'd love him if he were a pauper. Though, finding out they'd never have to worry about financial security was a really nice thing to know.

"Wow." She didn't know what to say, really. He'd just stunned her.

He squeezed her waist as he looked down at her, grinning. "Are you impressed? Do you like the idea of marrying a rich husband?"

"No, actually," she told him truthfully. "Though, I'll admit it's nice to know we won't have to worry about buying groceries. But I'm not happy about marrying a rich man, as you put it. I'm happy about marrying you, Den." Her tone turned serious as she gazed up into his eyes. "I love you."

Den kissed her, drawing out the kiss a lot longer than was

really acceptable in polite company, but if anybody tried to join them on the balcony, they quickly turned around and went back inside. When Den finally raised his head, their gazes met, and he was still smiling.

"I love you, too, Sunny."

*

Meanwhile, somewhere in Nebraska...

Even before he rose for the evening, the master vampire, Marco, sensed something stirring in the forest around the old mansion. He had begun the work of cleansing the place with the help of a nearby group of shapeshifters several months ago, and he still kept a close eye on it. It was empty now, but the mansion and its grounds had been used for terrible evil. The outside pavilion, in particular, had been drenched in blood magic, and the gardens around it had been seeded with evil gargoyle statues that came to life only to attack servants of the Light.

Marco might be limited to the hours of darkness because of his immortal nature, but he was a long-time servant of the Light, and an opponent of evil. He had spent many years watching over the mansion and grounds on the edge of his territory. He had rejoiced in helping rid the place of evil and then snatching it up when it was put up for sale. The place was finally his, but it remained a problem. It was empty when the work crews went home, and the echoes of the evil that had been done there reverberated.

What the estate really needed was new inhabitants. Good people with good plans for the place. He just hadn't found any to take it over yet.

And now, he wasn't sure it would be safe to do so. Something was going on there, and he needed to find out what it was. If evil had returned to the estate, he was going to have to do something about it.

Please enjoy this excerpt from the next book in the series:

Brotherhood of Blood ~ Wildwood 2

NIGHT OF THE NYMPH

Chapter One

Even before he rose for the evening, the master vampire of this region, Marco, sensed something stirring in the forest around the old mansion. He had begun the work of cleansing the place with the help of a nearby group of shape shifters several months ago and he still kept an eye on it. It was empty now, but the mansion and its grounds had been used for terrible evil. The outside pavilion, in particular, had been drenched in blood magic, and the gardens around it had been seeded with evil gargoyle statues that came to life only to attack servants of the Light.

Marco might be limited to the hours of darkness because of his immortal nature, but he was a long time servant of the Light, and an opponent of evil. He had spent many years watching over the mansion and grounds on the edge of his territory, in eastern Nebraska. He had rejoiced in helping rid the place of evil. But, it remained a problem. It was empty and the echoes of the evil that had been done there reverberated.

What the place really needed, was new inhabitants. Good people with good plans for the place. He just hadn't found any to take it over, yet.

And now, he wasn't sure it would be safe to do so. Something was going on there, and he needed to find out what it was. If evil had returned to the mansion, he was going to have to do something about it.

With that in mind, he rose in the darkness after twilight and headed out to check on the mansion. Although he was not strictly a mage, he had been able to forge some rudimentary wards around the property and those were being tested by something. He wasn't sure what. He also wasn't sure if it was good or evil. All he knew at this point, was that something had breached his wards, and he was going to find out who, or what, had done so, and why.

He flew through the night air in the form of a black dragon. As an ancient vampire, he had the strength to transform himself into just about any shape he desired. It wasn't shape shifting in the traditional sense. He wasn't like those who had a beast living in their soul and could only transform into that one animal. No, Marco could do just about any shape he could imagine. Even mist.

But he enjoyed the dragon form. He liked flying, and if he kept his size down to a reasonable stature, and his color very dark, then nobody could see him other than those with magic of their own. Regular people, those with no magic, never looked up when he passed over and didn't see him. Of course, he could influence their minds to look away and not notice him, as well, but he rarely had to resort to such methods.

As he flew over the forest that made up a large part of the mansion's property, he caught sight of something moving among the trees. He sensed magic, but it was a different sort than he was used to feeling. This felt almost...elemental. He couldn't be sure. He circled once again, then landed not far from where he had sensed the intruder.

Crystal had felt compelled to stop her car and enter the woodland that was crying out for help. It wasn't normal for her to do things like this, but she'd never felt a call so strongly. She had discovered an odd ability to hear the whispering, musical communication of trees long ago. She had always considered it a secret quirk that she never discussed with anyone, but she listened to the trees around her and learned many things.

She was on her way across the state for a job interview, but something had made her take the exit ramp and come to this lonely stretch of road. She'd stopped her car and rolled down the windows and a wave of despair came to her on the wind that nearly broke her heart.

Not really thinking about her actions, she'd gotten out of her car and walked into the woods, going deeper into the gloom as night fell. She wasn't afraid. The trees would warn her of any danger. They were her friends and would try to protect her. She didn't sense any wild animals that were big enough to hurt her or any other threats, but she felt the deep sorrow of the trees as a blow to her heart.

She summoned her energy and tried her best to soothe the trees, telling them that she was here and would do her best to help. She didn't know exactly what she could do, but she had to do *something*. It was a visceral need in her soul.

She walked among the trees, noting the presence of many oak and rowan seedlings that were doing their best to help their older friends of different varieties recover from whatever had been done to them and the land on which they grew. But the seedlings were too young and too much had happened here for them to be able to cleanse the land easily or quickly. It was going to be a really big job.

Crystal kept walking, not needing light to see as the sun went down. It was a quirk of her power that all living things gave off a slight glow that allowed her to see in the dark, as long as there were living things around her. She walked to the heart of the grove and sank down to her knees as the despair of the trees nearly overwhelmed her. They were all talking at once, as if they had been waiting for someone like her to arrive. Someone who could hear them.

The Protector comes. The trees whispered the phrase over and over, but she didn't know what it meant. She didn't feel endangered. Far from it. The trees liked this being—whoever the Protector was. She wasn't sure she should be here. She was trespassing, after all, but if the trees trusted this person, then perhaps she could convey to the Protector the need she felt from the trees for cleansing of the land.

She held her position. The Protector would either find her, or it wouldn't. She wasn't going to stop her work. She was busy summoning energy from the earth to cleanse the worst of the deep wounds suffered by the land in this area and, by association, the trees. It was the least she could do, and frankly, she couldn't go another moment listening to the wailing that only she could hear. The trees were in pain, and it pained her to hear it.

Master Marco flew overhead, making for the spot on the edge of the forest nearest the road where he saw a think golden glow through the trees. As he approached, the golden light shimmered, drawing him in like a moth to the flame. Intrigued, he circled, going lower to see if he could learn more before he landed, but the trees were too dense. He only got flickering images of a person standing in the center of the glow, seeming to command it with their hands.

It didn't look bad. It didn't feel evil. Instead, he got the impression that the being—whoever it was—wielded its power to try to help the forest in some way. Living things weren't his specialty. Especially not plants and trees. He had done what he could to try to help the land recover from the evil that had been done here. He had seeded the area with oak and rowan saplings, having heard that they naturally cleansed evil from the land.

Marco didn't know how long it would take, but time was something he had plenty of, and he often thought in terms of decades, or even centuries, rather than years or months. The little saplings were doing well. He checked on them regularly. But, he had no way of knowing how long it would take those brave little trees to overcome the horrors that had been committed on this land.

Maybe the trees had gotten tired of waiting. Maybe they had somehow summoned one who could help them faster. He'd heard rumors through the Masters network that ancient elemental powers were starting to show themselves once more in the mortal realm. Just recently, he'd been told by his old friend Hiram about a fierce battle involving four water elementals and a whole host of Others, including an entire town of bear shifters, assorted mages from different disciplines and heritages, someone with sylph blood and even a part-dryad.

They had managed, between them, to send a creature of evil back to its own realm of existence, before it could pollute the Earth's seas any more than it already had. If the creature had spawned here, for example, it would have meant centuries of incredibly powerful sea creatures—monsters, really—that would feed on any innocent traversing the oceans.

Hiram had nothing but praise for the people he had befriended in that new town in his territory that had sprung up a few years ago. Grizzly Cove was earning quite the reputation among magical folk. Both for the trouble it had encountered because of so much magic being gathered in such a small place, and for the social experiment of creating a town just for bear shifters, who normally roamed alone, or in small family groups.

Bear shifters weren't like werewolves. They didn't form Packs. At least, not usually. However, the Alpha who had created the town, had been a military leader. He had earned such respect and admiration from his men that they had followed him even into civilian life, and the town he had created for them all. If Marco ever found himself traveling again, he thought he would like to see this town called Grizzly Cove. Hiram's description made it sound like a very interesting place.

But Marco's traveling days were behind him. At least, that was his belief. He had picked this area of the country because there were few people, and even fewer of his kind. He had lived far beyond his expectations. Centuries of living had left him feeling morose, if he was being honest with himself. He was just existing. He was protecting his little part of the world against evil. That was his only goal in life, now. He had given up hoping for happiness, or a future with joy in it.

The years stretched ahead of him—and behind him—in a tedious line. He'd had an existential crisis of momentous proportions for a long time, until he just decided that he was here to protect his little area, and help where he could to stop evil from hurting anybody else the way it had hurt those he had cared for in the past. He wouldn't let himself in for that kind of pain again. He wouldn't form friendships with the mortals around him. He wouldn't harm them, of course, though he needed to feed from time to time, but he also wouldn't befriend them.

Losing them was too painful, especially when they succumbed to evil. It had happened both ways to him. Someone he had trusted had been turned to evil and broken his heart. Or, most often, evil targeted those he had befriended, killing them without remorse, in horrible ways. Either way, Marco ended up mourning. Grieving for the people he had lost over the many centuries he had been alive. The only thing keeping him going, at this point, was his responsibility to try to stem the tide of evil wherever he could, so that others wouldn't have to feel the soul-deep sadness he had felt too many times to remember.

He circled over the light, going lower on each pass, trying to discover what he could before he changed shape and landed among the trees. He couldn't very well land in his dragon form, even though he could be a man-sized dragon. The wingspan was always an issue among the tightly packed trees. But he didn't need wings to fly. He was vampire. He could become mist, if that's what he wanted. His magic was such that there was no limitation on the forms he could become, and flying was more of a magical operation than a mechanical one. At least, for him.

Maybe that wasn't the case for others of his kind. Marco didn't know for sure. He'd just always been able to do it, once he'd come fully into his power. That had happened sometime in the 1400s, when he had claimed mastery over his birth region in Italy, and he'd only grown incrementally stronger since then. Messina had been his birthplace, and also the site of the start of the Black Death in Europe when three ships docked there from the Black Sea, bringing the plague to his homeland.

He'd watched throughout, knowing the plague for what it was—a magical attack by the Destroyer—who wanted, insanely, to *cleanse* the world of non-magical humans to make way for her twisted idea of an evil empire. Elspeth had sent successive waves of disease and pestilence against innocent human beings over many years of struggle, when the forces of good tried so hard to gather their strength and fight her followers wherever they were found.

But Elspeth and her people, were cunning. They hid in the shadows and preyed on the innocent. They killed so many in their attempts to gain ultimate power. Eventually, the forces of good had won the day and sent Elspeth packing, imprisoned and exiled to the farthest realms. Her followers had been killed or disbanded, and her time was at an end.

Or, so they had thought. Her followers—the ancient order known as the *Venifucus*—had not disbanded, as he had believed for so long. In recent years, it had come to light that they had kept going in secret. They had been working all this time, to break Elspeth free of her prison and bring her back to the mortal realm.

Rumors abounded that they had in fact done just that. Marco wasn't sure, but he remained vigilant. He dreaded the idea that they would have to fight her all over again. He would do it. He wouldn't enjoy it, but he would do it. He had seen, firsthand, what she had done to the people of his beloved homeland and everyone else unfortunate enough to be in her path.

That's what kept him going. That was his reason for living. So few people alive today remembered what she had done. So few knew her tactics. He'd been a soldier on the side of Light. He knew what to expect from her and her people. It was his duty to be ready when his knowledge was needed again, and he very much feared that the time was drawing near.

Which was part of the reason he was so vigilant about this nearby mansion and its grounds. It had been fouled by blood magic and was susceptible to being misused again. He wouldn't let that happen. He had sworn to keep this place from being turned to evil once more. For lack of a better word, he was its caretaker. At least, until he could find people he could trust to inhabit the estate and watch over it for him.

The uninvited guest didn't seem to be doing anything bad. Marco would have sensed evil intent. He had set all sorts of spells and wards to warn him of just such an occurrence. When this person had crossed his ward, it had not flared with alarm. It had alerted Marco to the presence of someone, but it had not sensed evil.

For that matter, Marco didn't sense any evil, either. He was intrigued, as he floated to earth, landing, by design, about twenty yards away from the glowing golden light. He wanted time to study the person at the center of the light. He intended to approach slowly, learning all he could as he drew closer, step by step.

Crystal sobbed as she reached for the earth energy, trying to cleanse what she could of the evil that permeated the ground here. It felt like some sort of blood magic had been soaked into every pebble, every grain of sand, every molecule of earth that surrounded the root systems of its suffering trees. It hurt so bad. It hurt the trees. It hurt the land. It hurt her to be in contact with it, but she must. She had to try.

Everything around her cried out for her help, but she had never faced anything this profound before. She'd never been so immersed in so much death and decay. Crystal began to doubt herself. She didn't know if she could handle this, but she had to try something. She couldn't just leave it this way. She couldn't just run away and pretend she'd never seen this blight.

Reaching deep within herself, she tapped the energy that lived within her soul. She had done it before, on a much smaller scale, to help save the life of dying plants. She knew she could give a little bit of herself to bring the plant back to life. She wondered if she could do the same here.

She would have to be careful. As far as she understood it,

the power she used came from within herself. She couldn't leave herself too weak to walk, or drive away. She had to have that out. If she opened herself up completely, this place might drain her dry and leave her comatose, or worse.

That in mind, she tried really hard to channel just a little bit of her energy into her hands. It manifested as a golden ball of light, glowing strong in the gloom of the forest night. She felt a little shaky. Maybe she had taken a little too much at one time, but she was committed now. She had to redirect the golden energy from her hands, down into the earth. She believed it would cleanse whatever it came into contact with, relieving some of the pain she sensed all around.

She knew she couldn't do much with just her own energy, but it was all she had to give. She wasn't very skilled with this sort of thing, having taught herself the little she knew. There just wasn't anyone around who had the same kind of power she seemed to have. She'd asked—very cautiously, of course. She'd talked to many people who claimed to know about the magic of the earth, but nobody had really been able to give her the knowledge she felt she needed. So, she had experimented. Trial and error had been her constant companion these past few years since she had discovered the energy within herself.

She really hoped this wasn't going to be one of the *errors*. Sending a quick prayer aloft, she sank to one knee and placed one palm down on the ground transferring the golden ball of light from her hands into the earth.

"Oh, boy…" She had a moment of wobbly awareness that she'd gone just a little too far before she slumped, unconscious, to the ground.

To read more, get your copy of

Night of the Nymph by Bianca D'Arc.

ABOUT THE AUTHOR

Bianca D'Arc has run a laboratory, climbed the corporate ladder in the shark-infested streets of lower Manhattan, studied and taught martial arts, and earned the right to put a whole bunch of letters after her name, but she's always enjoyed writing more than any of her other pursuits. She grew up and still lives on Long Island, where she keeps busy with an extensive garden, several aquariums full of very demanding fish, and writing her favorite genres of paranormal, fantasy and sci-fi romance.

Bianca loves to hear from readers and can be reached through Twitter (@BiancaDArc), Facebook (BiancaDArcAuthor) or through the various links on her website.

WELCOME TO THE D'ARC SIDE...
WWW.BIANCADARC.COM

OTHER BOOKS BY BIANCA D'ARC

Brotherhood of Blood
One & Only
Rare Vintage
Phantom Desires
Sweeter Than Wine
Forever Valentine
Wolf Hills*
Wolf Quest

Brotherhood ~ Wildwood
Dance of the Dryad
Night of the Nymph
Wildwood in Winter
The Elven Star

Tales of the Were
Lords of the Were
Inferno
Rocky
Slade

Tales ~ String of Fate
Cat's Cradle
King's Throne
Jacob's Ladder
Her Warriors

Tales ~ Redstone Clan
The Purrfect Stranger
Grif
Red
Magnus
Bobcat
Matt

Tales ~ Grizzly Cove
All About the Bear
Mating Dance
Night Shift
Alpha Bear
Saving Grace
Bearliest Catch
The Bear's Healing Touch
The Luck of the Shifters
Badass Bear
Bounty Hunter Bear
Storm Bear
Bear Meets Girl
Spirit Bear
Lion in Waiting
Black Magic Bear
Wolf Tracks

Tales ~ Trident Trilogy
Waterborn
Fathom
Leviathan

Tales ~ Were-Fey
Lone Wolf
Snow Magic
Midnight Kiss

Tales ~ Lick of Fire
Phoenix Rising
Phoenix and the Wolf
Phoenix and the Dragon

Tales ~ Big Wolf
A Touch of Class
Perfect
The Werewolf Alpha's
Solstice Miracle

Tales ~ Jaguar Island
The Jaguar Tycoon
The Jaguar Bodyguard
The Jaguar's Secret Baby
The Jaguar Star

Guardians of the Dark
Simon Says
Once Bitten
Smoke on the Water
Night Shade
Shadow Play

Gifts of the Ancients
Warrior's Heart
Future Past
A Friend in Need
Heal the Healer

Tales ~Gemini Project
Tag Team
Doubling Down
Deuces Wild

Resonance Mates
Hara's Legacy**
Davin's Quest
Jaci's Experiment
Grady's Awakening
Harry's Sacrifice

Dragon Knights
Daughters of the Dragon
Maiden Flight*
Border Lair
The Ice Dragon**
Prince of Spies***

The Novellas
The Dragon Healer
Master at Arms
Wings of Change

Sons of Draconia
FireDrake
Dragon Storm
Keeper of the Flame
Hidden Dragons

The Sea Captain's Daughter
Book 1: Sea Dragon
Book 2: Dragon Fire
Book 3: Dragon Mates

The Captain's Dragon
Snow Dragon
Gatekeeper

Jit'Suku Chronicles
Arcana
King of Swords
King of Cups
King of Clubs
King of Stars
End of the Line
Diva

StarLords
Hidden Talent
Talent For Trouble
Shy Talent

Jit'Suku Chronicles
Sons of Amber
Angel in the Badlands
Master of Her Heart

Jit'Suku Chronicles
In the Stars
The Cyborg Next Door
Heart of the Machine

StarLords
Hidden Talent
Talent For Trouble
Shy Talent

Irish Lullaby
Bells Will Be Ringing
Wild Irish Rose

More than Mated
The Right Spot

* RT Book Reviews Awards Nominee
** EPPIE Award Winner
*** CAPA Award Winner

Welcome to Grizzly Cove, where bear shifters can be who they are - if the creatures of the deep will just leave them be. Wild magic, unexpected allies, a conflagration of sorcery and shifter magic the likes of which has not been seen in centuries... That's what awaits the peaceful town of Grizzly Cove. That, and love. Lots and lots of love.

This series begins with...

All About the Bear

Welcome to Grizzly Cove, where the sheriff has more than the peace to protect. The proprietor of the new bakery in town is clueless about the dual nature of her nearest neighbors, but not for long. It'll be up to Sheriff Brody to clue her in and convince her to stay calm—and in his bed—for the next fifty years or so.

Mating Dance

Tom, Grizzly Cove's only lawyer, is also a badass grizzly bear, but he's met his match in Ashley, the woman he just can't get out of his mind. She's got a dark secret, that only he knows. When ugliness from her past tracks her to her new home, can Tom protect the woman he is fast coming to believe is his mate?

Night Shift

Sheriff's Deputy Zak is one of the few black bear shifters in a colony of grizzlies. When his job takes him into closer proximity to the lovely Tina, though, he finds he can't resist her. Could it be he's finally found his mate? And when adversity strikes, will she turn to him, or run into the night? Zak will do all he can to make sure she chooses him.

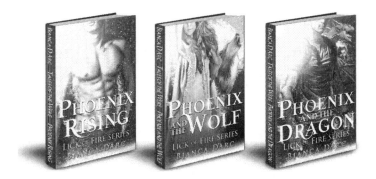

Phoenix Rising

Lance is inexplicably drawn to the sun and doesn't understand why. Tina is a witch who remembers him from their high school days. She'd had a crush on the quiet boy who had an air of magic about him. Reunited by Fate, she wonders if she could be the one to ground him and make him want to stay even after the fire within him claims his soul...if only their love can be strong enough.

Phoenix and the Wolf

Diana is drawn to the sun and dreams of flying, but her elderly grandmother needs her feet firmly on the ground. When Diana's old clunker breaks down in front of a high-end car lot, she seeks help and finds herself ensnared by the sexy werewolf mechanic who runs the repair shop. Stone makes her want to forget all her responsibilities and take a walk on the wild side...with him.

Phoenix and the Dragon

He's a dragon shapeshifter in search of others like himself. She's a newly transformed phoenix shifter with a lot to learn and bad guys on her trail. Together, they will go on a dazzling adventure into the unknown, and fight against evil folk intent on subduing her immense power and using it for their own ends. They will face untold danger and find love that will last a lifetime.

Lone Wolf

Josh is a werewolf who suddenly has extra, unexpected and totally untrained powers. He's not happy about it - or about the evil jackasses who keep attacking him, trying to steal his magic. Forced to seek help, Josh is sent to an unexpected ally for training.

Deena is a priestess with more than her share of magical power and a unique ability that has made her a target. She welcomes Josh, seeing a kindred soul in the lone werewolf. She knows she can help him... if they can survive their enemies long enough.

Snow Magic

Evie has been a lone wolf since the disappearance of her mate, Sir Rayburne, a fey knight from another realm. Left all alone with a young son to raise, Evie has become stronger than she ever was. But now her son is grown and suddenly Ray is back.

Ray never meant to leave Evie all those years ago but he's been caught in a magical trap, slowly being drained of magic all this time. Freed at last, he whisks Evie to the only place he knows in the mortal realm where they were happy and safe—the rustic cabin in the midst of a North Dakota winter where they had been newlyweds. He's used the last of his magic to get there and until he recovers a bit, they're stuck in the middle of nowhere with a blizzard coming and bad guys on their trail.

Can they pick up where they left off and rekindle the magic between them, or has it been extinguished forever?

Midnight Kiss

Margo is a werewolf on a mission...with a disruptively handsome mage named Gabe. She can't figure out where Gabe fits in the pecking order, but it doesn't seem to matter to the attraction driving her wild. Gabe knows he's going to have to prove himself in order to win Margo's heart. He wants her for his mate, but can she give her heart to a mage? And will their dangerous quest get in the way?

The Jaguar Tycoon

Mark may be the larger-than-life billionaire Alpha of the secretive Jaguar Clan, but he's a pussycat when it comes to the one women destined to be his mate. Shelly is an up-and-coming architect trying to drum up business at an elite dinner party at which Mark is the guest of honor. When shots ring out, the hunt for the gunman brings Mark into Shelly's path and their lives will never be the same.

The Jaguar Bodyguard

Sworn to protect his Clan, Nick heads to Hollywood to keep an eye on a rising star who has seen a little too much for her own good. Unexpectedly fame has made a circus of Sal's life, but when decapitated squirrels show up on her doorstep, she knows she needs professional help. Nick embeds himself in her security squad to keep an eye on her as sparks fly and passions rise between them. Can he keep her safe and prevent her from revealing what she knows?

The Jaguar's Secret Baby

Hank has never forgotten the wild woman with whom he spent one memorable night. He's dreamed of her for years now, but has never been back to the small airport in Texas owned and run by her werewolf Pack. Tracy was left with a delicious memory of her night in Hank's arms, and a beautiful baby girl who is the light of her life. She chose not to tell Hank about his daughter, but when he finally returns and he discovers the daughter he's never known, he'll do all he can to set things right.

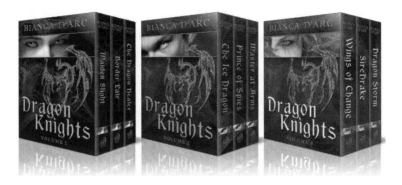

Dragon Knights

Two dragons, two knights, and one woman to complete their circle. That's the recipe for happiness in the land of fighting dragons. But there are a few special dragons that are more. They are the ruling family and they are half-dragon and half-human, able to change at will from one form to another.

Books in this series have won the EPPIE Award for Best Erotic Romance in the Fantasy/Paranormal category, and have been nominated for *RT Book Reviews Magazine* Reviewers Choice Awards among other honors.

WWW.BIANCADARC.COM

Made in United States
Orlando, FL
27 December 2022